MUSINGS

MUSINGS
a short story collection

ALYCIA CHRISTINE

Purple Thorn Press
www.purplethornpress.com

"Sumari's Solitude" by Alycia C. Cooke first published in RUINS METROPOLIS anthology, Hadley Rille Press, 2008. Copyright © 2008 by Alycia C. Cooke

"Raven's Fall" by Alycia C. Cooke first published at Confabule.com, 2013. Copyright © 2013 by Alycia C. Cooke

"Chosen Sacrifice" by Alycia C. Cooke first published at AlyciaChristine.com, 2013. Copyright © 2013 by Alycia C. Cooke

"A Song for Naia" by Alycia Christine first published at Smashwords.com, 2014. Copyright © 2014 by Alycia Christine

"Of Kelpie Lullabies" by Alycia C.Cooke first published at Smashwords.com, 2014. Copyright © 2014 by Alycia C. Cooke

Preface, Stories, and Commentaries Copyright © 2014 by Alycia Christine

Cover illustration and design by Alycia Christine
Cover Copyright © 2014 by Purple Thorn Press

First Purple Thorn Press trade paperback edition published 2014.
Printed by CreateSpace.

Alycia Christine
http://www.AlyciaChristine.com

Purple Thorn Press
http://www.PurpleThornPress.com

ISBN 978-1-941588-11-6

Through laughter and tears, thank you, my sweet Rebekah, for chasing the rabbit trails with me all these years.

Musings Contents

Preface...13

Musings *poetry*..17

Sumari's Solitude *fiction*...19
Sumari's Solitude: A Deeply Personal Adventure *commentary*........36

Star Child and the Golden Seed *fiction*...38
Star Child and the Golden Seed: A Story of Faith *commentary*.......42

The Soul Wrangler *fiction*..43
The Soul Wrangler: A Duel between Good and Evil *commentary*.....56

My Hero, His Monster *poetry*...59

What Tendrils Echo *fiction*...63
What Tendrils Echo: The Siren Song of Power *commentary*..........84

City of Twilight *fiction*..85
City of Twilight: The First Short Story *commentary*......................94

My Love for Thee *poetry*...97

Raven's Fall *fiction*..99
Raven's Fall: Mythology Takes Flight *commentary*.......................102

The Banner Prophesies *fiction*...103
The Banner Prophesies: A Parent's Ultimate Act of Love *commentary*..........107

Winter Winds Blow *poetry*...109

A Song for Naia *fiction*..111
A Song for Naia: A Trial of Frost and Fire *commentary*................114

Musings Contents

Winter's Charge *fiction*..115
Winter's Charge: The Journey between Hatred and Peace *commentary*.......130

You Are More *poetry*...133

Chosen Sacrifice *fiction*...135
Chosen Sacrifice: The Honor of Forgiveness *commentary*...............................146

Of Kelpie Lullabies fiction...148
Of Kelpie Lullabies: The Choice of Redemption *commentary*.....................159

Acknowledgements...163
Author Interview...165
Also by Alycia Christine...171
Meet the Author..173

Preface

Shortly after I began writing speculative fiction, I received some sage advice from acclaimed Dragonriders of Pern series author Todd McCaffrey: don't neglect the short story. I was working on the rough draft of my first novel at the time and wondered why I should stop what I was doing to focus on other smaller projects. Weren't novels more popular and didn't they gain their creators more money? Why bother with the short story?

Eight years later and I think I finally understand his counsel. Short stories are a proving ground for writers. If I, as an author, can first achieve success through writing a short story, then it is much easier for me to take the skills well learned and translate them into a longer fiction form. Thus a powerful short story can sometimes build an author's career faster than a novel because its smaller word count takes less time to write, but also makes each word used in building the tale more important.

This anthology marks my first comprehensive attempt to honor the short form. I have included eleven short stories amassed from eight years of literary experimentation. Each tale represents a step in my journey as a speculative fiction writer thus far: from the first tumbled words of 2006 to the published triumphs of "Sumari's Solitude" in 2007 and "Raven's Fall" in 2013. Some tales are stories nestled in the larger worlds also populated by my books while others are meant to stand alone as single flames representing the overall bonfire of my imagination. Their sizes range as well: from flash fiction told in as little as 900 words to stories in excess of 7,500 words. While some of these short stories have seen previous publication, Musings marks the first public appearance for many.

In one way or another, each of these tales represents a different aspect of who I am as a person and what I have experienced during my lifetime. I have therefore included an explanation of what prompted my scribbled exploration of each story idea at the end of each piece of fiction.

Finally there are five poems designed to further the emotional depth of the book and bridge the gap between certain stories. Some of these poems were written specifically for the book while others come from my personal poetry journal.

Thank you for reading my quiet musings. I hope this collection proves entertaining and thought-provoking for you. Until our next meeting, may we each rewrite our world for the better.

Musings

Butterflies float over cracked earth
Along a creek that is no more.
Their wings wink into twilight
Beyond the fractured far shore.

A dragon soars above me,
Its scarlet wings burning bright
As the last gold rays of sunlight
Guide it on into the night.

The fireflies greet me then
In the cool of autumn's day.
They add a touch of fairy light
To the streaming Milky Way.

I sit beneath the thorn tree
And gaze at the purple sky.
There between sand and starlight
All my musings finally fly.

Sumari's Solitude

Sumari stood near the balcony's sheltering pillar watching the breath of the gods make living waves of the sand dunes beyond Aamanru Temple. Her small right hand kept her dark veil in check while the left fist held the deep opening of her indigo robes firmly closed to shield her gold pendant and tattoo from the dancing dust. She huddled near the warmth of an alabaster lamp and sadly watched the sun, Aa's eye, descend into the desert.

"High Priestess?" a male's voice hissed.

She turned away from the sunlit sands and beheld a lamia guard watching her curiously.

"King Draigoss has arrived, Mistress," he said, bowing low. "You are needed at the front entry."

She watched him with bemusement, wondering how he could actually balance well enough on his scaly tail to demonstrate such an act of respect toward her.

"Very well, Kaa, I shall greet him. Have you said your evening prayers yet?"

The strapping snake-man shook his human-like head. "No, Mistress, but I shall once I escort you to the main hall."

She smiled. "Very well then…to the task at once. We should not keep the exalted Sathe or the good king waiting."

Kaa grinned, exposing his sharp fangs, and then slithered protectively after the high priestess—his Iklwa spear gripped firmly with both hands. The human and lamia wound their way around the inscribed sandstone monoliths supporting the temple's vaulted ceiling and finally descended the stone steps leading to the main hall where Draigoss and his entourage waited.

19

"Good evening to you, Sire!" Sumari said as she formally curtseyed. "What brings you to my humble hovel?"

Draigoss returned her bow and, although his bearded lips twitched at her ironic statement, he said formally, "A pleasure as always to greet you, High Priestess Sumari. Forgive me, but I am in need of your generous assistance."

"I freely give it as always, Your Majesty. But first, let me see to the comfort of your companions…Kaa, have the slaves prepare fourteen east wing chambers for our guests."

"It will be done, Mistress." Kaa put his right fist to his heart in salute and bowed before leaving.

"Ryald," she said, turning to another temple guard, "show our guests to the formal dining den and give them whatever sustenance they require."

"At once, Mistress!" The other lamia guard saluted her and bowed before clapping his hands together. Slaves slipped from the pillars' shadows and carried Draigoss's companions' belongings to their chambers while Ryald politely motioned the guests through an archway and down a side hall toward the kitchen and dining areas.

The king did not follow his party, but instead stood watching his aides and personal guards march down the corridor. He then turned to the High Priestess of Aa.

"I am sorry over the appalling length between visits," he murmured. "Affairs of state have kept me away from this hallowed ground and your honored presence for far too long."

"Indeed your presence has been most missed," Sumari replied perfunctorily. "Come. If you wish it, we may talk privately in my study after I call for some tea."

The king nodded and so she motioned him to ascend the redstone stairs with her. They did not speak again until Sumari had led him through the labyrinth of hallways to her private chambers. After she had sent the chamber slave to the kitchens for herb tea and fruit, Sumari shed her formal headdress and veil with relief.

"Sumari…" the king whispered and pulled her into his arms before she could breathe.

"No, Draigoss! We mustn't!" she said, pushing away from him.

"Please, My Pearl, let me hold you a moment for my sagacity's sake."

Sumari finally relented and felt the comfort of his strong arms encompass her small body. He held her protectively, running calloused brown fingers gently through her ebony tresses.

"I missed you so," she quaked against the dusty robes covering his broad chest.

"I know...I missed you, too," he whispered before kissing her forehead. They stood there embracing until the scratch of scales against stone alerted them that the chamber slave had returned with their tea. By the time the slave had opened the door, the monarch and priestess were comfortably seated on opposite divans and engaged in a spirited conversation about state politics.

"Thank you, Mynza," Sumari said when the female had poured cups for Draigoss and herself. She dismissed the female who bowed and slithered out of the room.

The priestess signaled to Draigoss in formal hand-sign language: "No doubt she'll have her ear pinned against the door."

"Indeed," he signed back to her.

"Mynza!" the priestess called more loudly than necessary.

The young female lurched through the door looking abashed.

"Summon Kaa, please. You will find him either overseeing the preparations of the east wing bedchambers or at prayer. You will wait until he is finished with his tasks and then bring him to me."

Mynza looked disappointed but affirmed her instructions and left.

"Nicely done," Draigoss murmured.

Sumari smiled, then became serious. "All right, Draigoss, I know this isn't a purely social visit. What has happened to make you travel such a distance?"

The king nodded grimly. "An alarming report has reached me that certain members of the priesthood plan to foil the Conversion Ceremony and possibly assassinate whomever you pick as successor."

Sumari sat up and sighed. "And Makili is among the conspirators."

"How did you know?"

"I have my sources too, Draigoss." Sumari's eyes narrowed dangerously. "They must think that I will appoint a woman to succeed me."

"Precisely. You have made many enemies during your de-cade-long reign as Aa's most faithful servant. Many of the priests believe that the leadership of Aamanru Temple and the surround-ing oasis of Daku is better left in male control."

"It is not their decision!" the priestess growled. "It's not even my decision! Aa chooses whom he wishes to serve him however he sees fit. I have no more control over that than Makili or his cohorts."

"I know, Pearl, I know."

Sumari rose and began to pace the room. "The time of deci-sion draws near; in four days I must go into seclusion and com-mune with Aa during Solitude. Hopefully, he will have the an-swers I seek and offer us protection against those who would betray our faith."

"I hope so...for all of our sakes..." Draigoss sniffed his tea critically. "Do you not have something besides rooibos? I could do with a good stout black tea."

Sumari smiled at the familiar complaint. "You know other tea plants cannot grow in our soils. It is rooibos or nothing."

Draigoss made a face and then downed his cup's steaming contents in three gulps before starting to sate his appetite with the tray of fruit. Sumari sat again and shared the plate with him, content to avoid discussing religious politics for the present. She must deal with such unpleasant matters too soon anyway.

***

Kaa knocked once and then glided into Sumari's study. "It is time, High Priestess. All is prepared for Solitude."

"Thank you, Kaa."

Sumari slowly rose off the divan and, after rearranging her simple white garments, she followed Kaa out of her chambers and down the corridor. The temple's central sanctuary was deco-rated with extra torches, incense spirals, and fragrant flowers in honor of Sumari's impending Solitude.

All of Daku's priests and priestesses had gathered to watch her ascend the steps of the Watch Tower ruins and commune with their god. Many murmured prayers or blessings as Sumari passed. Some muttered darkly to each other. All ogled her bra-zenly. Sumari stood straight amidst so many eyes and kept a stately gait. She paused on the dais at the center of the room and addressed the crowd.

"Today I enter Solitude as a pilgrim summoned by Aa. I go to him under the laws governing us set forth by the gods, and I shall return the same—not as a woman or a priestess, but as his humble servant. I go to seek a blessing from Aa for all who live in his service. May he find me worthy of his attendance and honor me with the name of the one he favors as my successor!"

The crowd cheered and Sumari turned toward the doorway leading to the half-ruined steps of the ancient Watch Tower. She paused only when she glimpsed Draigoss, and her hand subtly flicked a goodbye to him. She then turned to the crowd once more and bowed as deeply as a slave toward them. Cheers followed her ascent up the stairs.

Once she finally crossed the threshold of Aa's meeting room at the top of the tower, two priests set her provisions inside and sealed the room's door from the outside. The high priestess could not leave the tower for seven days and could consume food only for the first four. During the final three days, Sumari would perform the ceremonial fast—abstaining from food during her heaviest prayer period.

Although she knew the rules associated with it, Sumari had never before undertaken a full Solitude. The ritual itself was only performed in its entirety once a change in high priest was required. Sumari, the first high priestess in Aamanru's history, had been chosen by her predecessor, High Priest Qumar, through this rite. She had learned much from him in her first years at the temple and credited most of her present wisdom to his patient tutelage. How she missed him these past ten years! Both he and Draigoss had been her steady anchors—Qumar before her ascension to full power and Draigoss during most of the last decade.

Sumari shook her head and tried to silence her unruly memories. She must focus her mind on the present task. Qumar had warned her that Solitude would be the greatest achievement of her career and the most beautiful yet terrifying experience of her life. Solitude acted as a time of introspection and judgment even as it filled the role of the first step in the transfer of priesthood power. According to Qumar, Aa could be quite harsh to his followers if they displeased him—especially his high priest. Sumari quaked before firmly regaining control of her fears and then stooped to the task of organizing her belongings. After she ate her evening meal, she knelt to watch Aa's eye descend into the desert beyond Daku Oasis.

After the shifting sands consumed the sun's last light, Sumari finished her prayer and turned toward her sleeping bundle with a sigh. Her sigh turned into a startled screech as she realized some-one else was in the stone room with her. Regaining her poise with slight difficulty, Sumari flushed with anger.

"How dare you disturb Solitude! None may enter here for seven days except my master!"

The man, if one could call him that, smiled. "Am I really so unfamiliar?"

Sumari looked critically at him in the growing darkness—tak-ing in his plain yet brilliant robes and his glowing golden skin. Her eyes widened in sudden recognition and the High Priestess of Aa fell upon her knees to rest her head on the prayer mat.

"Master!" she gasped.

"Peace, Sumari," Aa said and bent to gently raise her face to-ward his own. "I am sorry to startle you; however, it is better for me to appear in this form so that I do not blind you."

"So it is true that you are more brilliant than the sun in your true form?"

"Quite."

"I am sorry, Master; I did not expect you to come so soon! For-give my short-sightedness; of course you would appear when-ever you so desired!"

"Peace, child! I came not to scold you, but to counsel you. Come, sit and commune with me."

The priestess nodded slightly and sat on the edge of her rug opposite her god. She looked upon him in awe, again noting the contrast between his commanding presence and his humble vis-age.

"How may I serve you, Mighty Aa?" she asked with a smile.

"It is I who will serve you tonight, Devoted Sumari," Aa said, returning her smile. "Of late, there have been many changes among the gods' hierarchy. The other gods remain loyal to me and continue in their faithful service. Some serve me out of fear, most serve out of love, but blessed Sathe bases his devotion on the great debt which he owes me."

Sumari nodded. "This I know. Honored Sathe owes his very divinity to you because you saved him from demotion and death at the vile hands of the god Nune."

"Correct. And Nune will eternally remain a prisoner of the soul-devourer Theibu as reward for his treachery."

Sumari nodded again and Aa looked seriously at his disciple. "Sathe has cheerfully served as my bondservant for many centuries now—just as his children are willing slaves to my humans. Over the years he and I have grown close, and Sathe is more like a brother to me now. I have decided to annul his life-debt because I believe him finally wise enough to appreciate his freedom. However, his release from bondage comes at a great cost since it will cause terrible strife among our disciples."

Sumari tilted her head slightly and studied her master's face—waiting for him to verbalize the concern his eyes conveyed.

Aa frowned. "I am afraid that both humans and lamia are far too stubborn to change the way their societal hierarchy has always existed, so I must do it for them."

"You mean to free the lamia slaves!"

Aa again nodded. "I have been guiding events for more than a century to push the two societies toward this great change and I now believe the time is ripe for the lamia to live as freely as their patron god. Sathe agrees with me and will help shepherd his people as they make the necessary transitions. I will set the example for my children with my next choice of high priest or priestess."

"Master, there will be riots if I announce for you that the slaves are free!"

"I know. This is why I shall descend the tower steps with you in six days and make the announcement myself."

"You would reveal yourself directly to the priesthood?"

"With a decision like this, I believe I should. Of late, my disciples have become dispirited and suspicious of my judgments. I wish to assuage the fears of the faithful and silence the doubters. Do not worry; those who naysay my words will face the wrath of my Sun-bearer."

"That could be every priest and priestess in Aamanru, especially if Makili and his cronies can stir up the crowd! You must know that they already conspire against your choice of my successor!"

The god's mouth hardened. "Then they will be the first to feel my judgment."

Sumari bowed. "As you wish, My Lord."

Aa smiled gently again. "We will discuss such matters in more detail subsequently. Now, tell me...how fares Draigoss? I have noticed far more tenderness growing between the two of you of late."

Sumari's cheeks burned. "Master, forgive me! I have tried to do your will and devote myself only to you but...I have failed. Draigoss is such a dear friend to me and...now I..."

"You love him."

Sumari hung her head in misery. "Yes, I do."

"Be still, be still!" the sun god almost laughed. "I do not despise such affection! Truly love is life's purest blessing. Even the gods covet it! You both have chosen well to love one another and yet not taint such beauty with physical lust. For that I thank you. I will soon reward you both for your devotion to me and to each other. You have served me well over these past years and you have shepherded my flock admirably despite some frustrating interference. I am most pleased with you, Sumari. Now, come and sleep. I will visit you again tomorrow evening once my task of watching this portion of the world is finished."

Sumari bowed and reverently kissed Aa's robes before obediently curling up in her blankets against the wall of the circular room. She saw nothing but darkness after the glowing god disappeared. A dreamless sleep took her then and she knew nothing until Aa's eye gazed upon her at dawn.

***

For six days Sumari had felt utter peace. She used daylight to read the sacred scrolls, pray, sing hymns to her god, or stare out across the sands and trace the path of Aa's fiery eye as it moved across the sky. When darkness fell, Aa would light the ancient Watch Tower with his presence and talk with her for hours about both mortal and immortal affairs. Their meetings were bliss.

When the seventh and final day of Solitude dawned, however, the High Priestess of Aa cringed. Today must be the day of Aa's Emancipation and Sumari felt apprehension gnaw at her spirit. She pushed back the sleeping blankets and ran to the tower's east window to search for the comforting sun, but it was not there. Although Sumari knew that morning had come, the sun was nowhere in sight and darkness still covered the landscape.

"Do not worry; all is well," a familiar voice said behind her.

Sumari turned and bowed to Aa, who seemed somewhat diminished in glow this day.

"Master, why does your eye not gaze upon the world today?"

"Because I gaze upon it in the full flesh today, Sumari. As I said, do not worry. I have left Sathe in charge of watching the world today and he does so even now," the god said while pointing to the moon still peeking over the horizon.

An astonished Sumari bowed to the moon and then bowed again to Aa.

"Come, Sumari. We will leave Nune's old tower and return to my temple just as soon as Sathe sends my Sun-bearer to us."

"Master, a question...why did you decide to have your disciples build your temple over the ruins of Nune's old fortress and yet leave his ruined Watch Tower standing as your personal meeting place with mortals?"

"A wise question, Sumari. Why do you think I would do such a thing?"

The priestess paused pensively and then answered, "Was destroying the fortress and building the temple over it a way to bury Nune's influence?"

The god sighed. "Partially, but it was actually more of an expedient way to cleanse the land of his pestilence. I blessed the land itself after razing Nune's palace and that is why the Oasis of Daku exists in the midst of the desert sands. Nune, of course, cursed the land and made it barren with his very presence, so I had to destroy all that he lay claim to so that the land would be fruitful again. I destroyed, blessed, and rebuilt the Watch Tower, however, as a testament to his evil so that I will never be tempted to grant him mercy. It also stands half-ruined as a reminder to both the gods and their disciples of greed's treachery."

"I see," Sumari said, looking around the simple stone structure, which was so unlike the opulence of Aamanru Temple.

"Good." Aa nodded in satisfaction. "Now come, my Sun-bearer approaches."

Sumari lifted her satchel onto a shoulder and followed Aa to the upper room's bolted door. The door yielded to the god's touch and they stepped onto the parapet and its descending stairs. A point of brilliant white light signaled the arrival of the Sun-bearer and Aa smiled as the winged unicorn circled once and then landed gracefully on the parapet beside them. The horse-like creature's iridescent feathers twinkled and his sharp golden horn glowed in the dim light.

"Sumari, you will descend first and bid the crowd to prostrate themselves in preparation for my visit. I will then enter, as is proper."

"Yes, Master!" The priestess bowed and hurried to comply with her god's orders. She knew that the priests and priestesses would not expect her to address them so soon and the priests guarding the bottom of the stairs indicated such when they both barred her from reaching the bottom step.

"High Priestess! This is most irregular! You should not be able to leave the tower until noon!"

"I am aware of the traditional end of Solitude, Sorak. However, Aa's message to our people will not wait…stand aside."

Neither Sorak nor his companion moved and their Iklwas stayed firmly crossed to thwart Sumari's advance.

"What is the meaning of this, Priest! I must do Aa's bidding!"

"There are those of us who believe that you would do your own bidding rather than our god's. I am sorry, Priestess, but you must wait until Makili finishes his address to the crowd, then you may defend yourself before the congregation and the Triad—"

"Triad!" Sumari shouted in rage. "I have committed no sin and he would put me before a Triad!"

"He addresses them as we speak," Sorak corrected her, growing bold. "You'll likely be put to death if the Triad finds you guilty of promiscuity. How long did you think we priests could turn a blind eye on your vile relationship with Draigoss?" Sorak spat. "That king has seduced you into doing his bidding and he will learn the consequences of his deceit, as will you."

"How dare you!" Sumari screeched. Before she could finish, however, Aa was there.

"Stand aside, Sorak," he said in a deadly voice. His usually bronzed face glowed crimson in fury.

The priest began to tremble violently and then fell to his face. His companion immediately discarded his weapon and also fell to his knees near the steps—his hands clasped in homage.

Aa bent and retrieved the two Iklwas and tested their blades' sharpness. He held Sorak's weapon toward his Sun-bearer. The unicorn sniffed it and whinnied softly as it shook its head. The god solemnly nodded and looked again toward the trembling man.

"My Sun-bearer smells no honest malice in your manner; however, I find your blatant disrespect of my highest disciple quite disturbing. Sorak, I am most disappointed in you."

The priest hid his face and began to sob.

"Notem, I find your faith complete; you shall be rewarded," Aa said gently to the other priest. "Stand and take up your Iklwa in defense of my name. Go tell the assemblage that I have finally come to counsel my people."

Notem stood at once, reverently took back his spear, and sprinted into the main sanctuary shouting wildly.

Sumari looked upon her god, who was still holding Sorak's Iklwa. As she watched, the unicorn tapped its spiraled horn to the weapon and it began to glow. The spear then lengthened and the blade reformed into the same symbol of Aa's eye that had been ceremonially tattooed onto Sumari's chest when she became the High Priestess of Aa.

"Take this and use it to protect yourself if need be," Aa said. "When the time is right, you will pass it and your pendant of office to your successor. Is that understood?"

"Yes, Master."

"Very good…now let us proceed. Notem will have the crowd disjointed by now and Makili will be most displeased." The god smirked.

Sumari strode purposefully into the sanctuary while her god and his Sun-bearer waited on the Watch Tower steps beside the still sobbing Sorak. The sight that next greeted her eyes was bedlam. Makili was standing on the center dais mopping his crimson brow with one hand while his other waved madly at the crowd before him. Everyone was talking at once, but all soon fell silent when they noticed Sumari standing with Aa's glowing staff clenched resolutely in her fist.

Priest Makili smiled as the crowd members regained composure, but his smirk turned cold as he saw Sumari. "So, our venerable high priestess would break Solitude before noon!"

"Remember to whom you so flippantly speak, Makili." Sumari strode to the dais and ascended its steps as she spoke. "As high priestess, I have the right to decide when our god's remarks are more important than tradition. I will address the crowd, Makili…

now." Her last word was punctuated by the staff's echoing ring as she brought it down on the dais stone.

Makili was furious but he still managed to mutter a barely polite "As you wish" before stepping down from the platform and taking his seat near the Triad members. Sumari watched him with barely restrained disgust before she looked upon the multitude.

"I come to you bearing this totem" —she held Aa's staff aloft— "as a sign of Aa's favor. Mark this day as one of joy for our god has chosen to reveal himself not only to me but to you as well—"

"And where is our god now, High Priestess?" Makili asked innocently.

"He waits and will appear once we show him proper reverence. I wish to lead you all in morning prayers..."

"You would attempt to lead worship, covered in sin as you are?" one crowd member shouted.

"Draigoss's whore has no authority over us!" another shouted.

Other slurs flew at her from throughout the throng. No doubt they were Makili's own cohorts planted amongst the people to stir them against her.

"Enough!" one of the Triad members demanded, cutting through the jeers. "High Priestess Sumari, please explain your declaration."

Sumari nodded and turned back to the crowd. "I have met with Aa these past days and communion with him was such a wonder. He told me many things, some of which were quite surprising. He believes the time is ripe for many changes to be made among his people and has bid me to prepare you all for his direct words. Aa and his Sun-bearer come this day—this very hour—to judge and reward the faithful." Sumari paused and turned back toward the Triad table. "Kind members of the Triad, I know that you are prepared to judge me for my actions this day. However, might it not be prudent to hold your deliberations until after our god makes his own remarks? I ask you only to judge me and those allied with me according to our god's own high standards."

Makili's mouth was slightly slack in shock as he seemed to realize that Sumari was freely giving herself up to judgment. She did not fight the initial appointment of the Triad, nor did she deny the charges set against her as he had evidently expected.

Sumari saw his eyes convey elation that his plans had come to easy fruition and yet suspicion that Sumari could yet hold some political weapon to thwart him. Clearly he did not believe her honest assertion that Aa would visit them in the flesh this day.

"If our great lord and master must come this day, let us not waste time with prosaic procedures..." Makili scoffed.

A second Triad member interrupted him. "Yes, let us indeed welcome him properly as our high priestess suggests."

Sumari nodded toward him with a small smile and turned toward the North entrance where she knew Aa was waiting. She stepped off the dais and bowed toward the door with her back to the crowd. The sounds of scraping shoes and rustling clothes filled the great room as the multitude behind Sumari followed her example. Even the Triad members left their stools and bowed down beside the judgment table.

"Mighty Aa lead us. Mighty Aa favor us. We are nothing. You are everything," everyone began to pray. "Mighty Aa lead us..."

As she chanted, Sumari lifted her head and banged the staff-butt against the ground to punctuate the chant's last words before repeating the prayer. With her staff-strike, a glowing figure swooped into the room and soared between the columns overhead. Several people—both priests and slaves—raised their heads to glimpse the figure and then quickly lowered their eyes to escape its brilliance. Aa and his flying steed circled above and then landed upon the dais just as the chant reached its climax. Then the unicorn's pealing neigh immediately silenced the crowd.

"Rise, my children, and look upon the face of your god!" Aa intoned.

As one, those in the crowd cautiously raised their heads and gasped as their gaze met his.

"I come with tidings of great import! Let every male and female be present...even those imprisoned within this temple must hear my words! Notem! Sorak!"

The two priests nervously stepped forward on opposite sides of the room.

"You and your subordinates will bring all those of the temple not currently in attendance to me at once! You will find stragglers and prisoners in the east wing and in the dungeons. Go!"

Notem and Sorak clapped their fists to their hearts and bowed low before running to their allotted task. Several priests and slaves hurried after them into the corridors beyond the main hall.

Aa slid off his steed's back and the Sun-bearer then stepped down to stand guard with Sumari just in front of the podium. The god and the crowd waited silently until the priests returned with the stragglers.

"Sumari," Aa murmured and bent down to gently touch her shoulder as he looked toward the prisoners.

The high priestess followed her god's gaze and gasped as she saw King Draigoss and his entourage in chains. The king's fine robes were ripped and his face was swollen with bruises.

"Who is responsible for this?" Sumari hissed in ire. "Explain yourself! How dare you lay a hand on the King of Patalia! Have you any idea what kind of war you've just brewed?"

Her god's gentle squeeze immediately silenced her.

"Makili gave the order, Sumari, just as he gave the order to arrest and try you after Solitude. He believes you and Draigoss offer a threat to his consolidation of power and he would rather be rid of you than have to plan around you."

"My Lord!" said Makili. "High Priestess Sumari and King Draigoss conspired against you...they, they have had improper relations while professing to honor you and—"

"Do you think me such a fool? Do you think I cannot see what my high priestess has and has not done with King Draigoss? They both have always put my wishes before their own passions even during the most difficult circumstances. I will amply reward them for their abstinence and devotion."

The god's visage smoldered as he looked toward the now cowering priest. "Makili, you have failed in your duties to me and to one whom I chose to rule over you! You knew full well the validity of Sumari's appointment as high priestess and yet you willfully deceived others against her. To disobey and discredit her, or any high priest, without proper moral evidence is to disrespect and rebel against me. You and your fellow conspirators must be judged."

Makili blanched and mopped his brow.

The god then looked upon his disciples. "Hear me, all of you! For those who unwisely followed Makili's orders and truly see the error of your ways, I forgive you. Do not stray from the path again. For those who do not truly repent, I will not shield you from the consequences of your foolishness!"

Sumari noticed several other priests throughout the throng shift uncomfortably where they knelt.

"My children, I have come to you this day to proclaim a monumental decree which will echo throughout future generations. I have decided to annul the god Sathe's life-debt to me. Because he has served me faithfully throughout so many human and lamia lifetimes, I feel that he has more than earned my respect and confidence. I have placed him in the Halls of the Heavens as my second eye—the night watcher and overseer. As Sathe is exalted, so shall I raise up his children. I hereby release the lamia from bondage—they are slaves no longer!"

Stunned silence followed by a worried murmur swept through the priesthood. Then the emancipated slaves began to laugh and cry and cheer. Aa's upheld hand silenced the throng once more.

"What I have decreed is law! May none who love me disobey. Sathe will shepherd his people through the transition between bondage and freedom. I ask that my priests and priestesses welcome the lamia as family just as I welcome Sathe as my brother. Who will obey me?"

Murmurs swept through the crowd again as Aa waited. Sumari stood scanning the crowd and then turned to her god.

"I will obey you, My Lord!" she declared, bowing.

Two of the Triad members stood and declared their loyalty, also bowing. They were followed by priest after priestess until almost all solemnly stood for their god. Sumari noted that Makili and his closest followers were among the few members of the multitude who still sat.

"Redeem yourself!" she hissed to him.

"And live in disgrace to you? Never!" Makili spat.

Sumari shook her head sadly and watched as her god did the same.

"This is your decision, then?" Aa asked the defiant priest.

Makili sat silently.

Aa nodded and then gazed upon the crowd once more. No more stood and so the god looked sadly at his steed and spoke. With his word the Sun-bearer leveled its horn with Makili's chest and a fireball sizzled from its spiraled point to pierce the priest's heart. The priest uttered a single tortured scream and then collapsed dead at the god's feet. The fire then leapt from the priest's chest and flew across the room, striking dead all those still sitting in defiance.

Aa bowed his head a moment and then spoke once more to his faithful. "Temple warriors, please remove the traitors from my sight!"

Lamia everywhere sprang into action and contemptuously hauled off the bodies. Kaa and Ryald were among the group set to remove Makili and the one defiant Triad member. But when they neared Aa, the god forbade Kaa to touch the body and ordered him to stay near Sumari instead.

Once the bodies were cleared and the guards had returned, the god finished his speech. "In light of the changes I have made, I will need strong leadership to see that all remain in harmony when I return to the sky. I therefore set the example for both gods and my children with my next choice of high priest. High Priestess Sumari please approach me and prepare to bestow your tokens of office upon your successor."

Sumari did as he commanded.

Aa then smiled gently, scanning the throng until his eyes rested on the lamia before him. "Kaa, approach me so that you may receive my blessings and take up your place as high priest and Sumari's rightful successor."

Gasps swept the crowd as the stunned lamia slithered up the steps of the dais. He stared in wonder from Sumari to Aa as the god took his Iklwa and Sumari gave him her staff. As Kaa precariously knelt to receive the pendant of office and have Sumari's tattoo of loyalty transferred to his own chest, the High Priestess of Aa swore she saw a tear glisten in the mighty warrior's eye.

***

Sumari stood against the marble railing of her bedroom balcony watching Aa's eye descend under the world and smiled. Many years of fond memories had been forged after Aa's Emancipation, but tonight her thoughts again rested with that seventh day of Solitude. The abolition of the lamias' slavery had come with the price of many lives in the Commoners' Rebellion following Aa's declaration, but the gods had mercifully helped both races come to harmony during the decade of Kaa's priesthood reign.

Sumari smiled again remembering the warrior-priest's joy the day his people became free.

The image triggered another memory full of Kaa's happy tears. To Sumari, the contemplation of this day was just as bittersweet as Aa's Emancipation because Aa had released Sumari from her priestess duties. She had been overjoyed when Aa attended the proceedings and had allowed Kaa to officiate during the unity ceremony, but she had been deeply saddened that she would no longer serve in the temple of her beloved god.

"Pearl, what are you thinking about?"

Sumari turned to see her husband and the father of her children smiling gently at her.

"Just remembering our wedding day," she said and returned his grin.

"That was an interesting day," Draigoss said wryly and laughed.

He walked to where his queen stood and pulled her into a hug as he watched the sunset over her slender shoulder. They stared smiling at the sky until the colors finally retreated to the advancing stars.

"Come…come to bed," Draigoss finally whispered.

He kissed his wife's neck before pulling her purposefully after him. They lay together embracing each other in the soft moonlight, content to adore one another under Sathe's gentle gaze as they had so many evenings before.

Sumari's Solitude:
A Deeply Personal Adventure

The start of my official fiction writing career began in 2007 when I sold my first short story "Sumari's Solitude" to Hadley Rille Books for distribution as the lead short story in the *Ruins Metropolis* anthology. Looking back at that short story now, I am extremely proud of that tale. Here is why: the story was the first short story that I had ever written that dealt with a deeply personal issue of mine.

My story's main character was the first female high priestess of her temple. Because of her spiritual and political position, she could not marry the man she loved. The tension of Sumari's occupation interfering with her love-life was one that I knew quite well. At the time of the story's writing, the man I loved and I were living over a thousand miles apart. I had moved to a new town with very few friends, I was working as the youngest reporter that my news publication had ever hired, and I was stuck in the middle of one of the most politically-charged offices I had ever encountered. I did not realize it at the time, but I desperately needed to vent my feelings about the whole maddening situation in a way that would not point fingers or fuel any gossip trains. Fiction writing became my answer.

I poured my conflicting feelings of frustration and longing and hope into the character of Sumari. I made her feel like a living, breathing person who shared some of my sorrows. The story's creation did not change my situation, but it did help me better cope with it. I wrote and edited the 6,000-word short story's manuscript in less than a month, a great feat for me in those days. It was accepted for publication by the first publisher to which I submitted it. I am now firmly convinced that one of the main reasons "Sumari's Solitude" was accepted for publication so quickly is because I poured a genuine piece of myself into its creation.

Star Child and the Golden Seed

Starlight spilled over the Watobi village's stone-and-sod huts, illuminating the face of every man, woman, and child as they watched the sky from beneath their homes' eaves. A winged white figure erupted out of the indigo expanse. Its descent stirred sudden whoops of joy from the besieged Watobi and fearful shrieks from the nearby Ankwa and Zubi encampments.

Village Elder Nebar watched the Stars' Gift's arrival with the memory of the old Star Sage's death still new in his mind. That death day had been early in the harvest when lightning had struck the Star Sage as he tried to protect the community's grain field from a storm's savagery. Without the sage's magic protecting the crop, the village's food supply was devoured by the lightning's fire. Thus they had no grain to pay their foes' demanded protection tribute when the Ankwa came to collect it.

This night of Stars' Gift marked the third week of siege by the allied Ankwa and Zubi tribes, whose leaders demanded Watobi slaves as compensation for the tribe's debts. The villagers had fought back and so far their defenses had held against the marauders' wind hammers. Yet Nebar knew their crumbling walls and courage would soon buckle under the mightier tribes' attacks. With little remaining hope, every member of the Watobi Tribe now gathered to scatter the dead sage's ashes upon the central Altar of Lilies and plead with his successor for a miracle.

They waited in silence as the bright figure lit upon the flower-shaped shrine and looked at the foot of the altar. The Watobi Tribe's youngest boy—who had lived only three harvests—lay cradled in a large straw basket below the incandescent being. The entity bowed once to the child host and then stooped to cradle him. The toddler returned the being's embrace and together they floated above the altar before the dead sage's ashes swirled up to cocoon them. A sound like a thunderclap marked the corporeal Star Child's first step out of the dissipating dust. Cheers erupted and the ebony-skinned villagers bowed as one when the hybrid of a child's innocence and the heavens' power stopped to study them.

"The late sage's totem is yours, Benevolent Successor," Nebar said as he humbly stepped forward to offer the staff of authority to the blue symbiont.

The new sage took the acacia staff and nodded his head once without blinking his ageless eyes. "What work must be done?"

"Honored Sage, our stores of food are spent and our enemies lurk in the shadow of our boundary walls ready to enslave our women and kill our children. If it pleases you, show mercy to your people. Drive our enemies from this place and reseed our lands with abundance."

The Star Child bowed his head in thought. "What you ask of me, I can do. Yet it would be more prudent for you to do such deeds yourself. For where does a man's strength lie if not within himself, bartered for by his own sweat? I will do what you ask, but you in turn must help me with the tasks I undertake."

"What would you have us do?" Nebar pleaded.

The Star Child retrieved a tiny golden seed from the sand at his bare feet and blessed it with a wave of his staff. In his small hand the seed began to multiply until there was a mound of many. He then instructed every leather-clad warrior to take a single seed from the pile.

"Now, tip your spears with these seeds washed in acacia sap. Once you have done this, prepare to attack the marauders at dawn before they can storm the village once more. You must drive your spears into the ground at their feet. You must not stab your enemies, only strike the earth. If even a single drop of their blood is spilled by Watobi hands, our foes will defeat us."

"What madness is this?" Nebar cried. "We will be slaughtered!"

"Upon my word and the force of my will, I vow you will not be harmed. But you must do as I say."

Nebar's head sagged in despair, but he obediently ordered the villagers to heed the Star Child's instructions.

***

Just before first sunlight, the Watobi prepared themselves for their last stand against their oppressors. The men of the tribe readied their weapons at the wall while the women sheltered the children inside the village's innermost huts.

With a wave of the Star Child's staff, the Watobi warriors poured over the stone bulwark and ran shouting in rage toward their would-be captors. Confused Ankwa and Zubi soldiers leapt from their sleeping furs to defend themselves against the tide of blue-painted tribesmen. Per the Star Child's order, every Watobi warrior sank a spear into the ground at his foe's feet before retreating to the wall. With each strike, a miracle occurred. The golden seeds immediately began to sprout and green herbs exploded out of the moist ground to wrap themselves around warriors' legs as they grew.

Screams from the tethered men woke the remaining sleepers and the allied camp was awash with crimson blood as orange-stained Zubi cut down both plants and green-swathed Ankwa in panic. The remaining tribesmen turned on each other and the Watobi warriors watched from the shelter of their wall as their enemies destroyed each other. In the end, no significant numbers of either tribe were alive to threaten the Watobi and so they retreated, leaving their dead to be devoured by the jackals.

"You have saved us!" Nebar exclaimed to his sage once the battle was won.

But the Star Child shook his head. "No, Nebar, you have saved yourselves. My brethren of the sky would never have chosen to allow me or my predecessors to bond with your people unless they were sure you could learn to improve yourselves. You may not be the strongest tribe on these plains, but you do have the most potential wisdom."

"I do not understand."

The Star Child pointed to the now verdant battleground. "Look at the fields you have planted for yourselves. There is enough growing now for a second harvest. You showed me faith, even if it was as small as the golden seeds you threw at your enemies. Still it grew like the seeds into an abundant belief, so now you and your families will reap the benefits of your obedience.

You now have a sturdy crop that will provide food, medicine, and flavorful spices for your meats. It will serve to nourish future generations of Watobi long after even I am gone."

Nebar stared in awe. "What is the magnificent plant's name, Honored Sage?"

The Star Sage's smile was gentle as he replied, "Mustard."

Star Child and the Golden Seed:
A Story of Faith

Human beings are capable of greatness, but sometimes we need a little supernatural help to nudge us on our way. This is the idea behind "Star Child and the Golden Seed." In writing this story, I really wanted to express the human need for faith and the rewards possible when faith in the right person is lived out wholeheartedly. As a young child, I loved reading Bible stories describing how faith in God helped different people overcome their troubles. Of particular interest to me were the Old Testament tales of the Israelites' constant reliance on God to help them vanquish much mightier foes.

These stories first planted the seeds of faith in my childhood mind, which blossomed into a simple practice of reliance upon someone wiser than myself to help me overcome my own problems: my parents, my teachers, and ultimately my savior Jesus Christ. It is these Old Testament tales coupled with the records of Jesus Christ's own miracles and discussions on faith that provide the framework for "Star Child and the Golden Seed."

My faith, of course, has grown in complication and has been redefined through the trials of age. But sometimes I have to remind myself that it is better to be a Watobi, living out a small seed of faith in something greater, than it is to rely on my own form of wisdom to get me through the day. So until the time that I actually have all the answers, will someone please pass the mustard?

The Soul Wrangler

Dust stared over the flat, cracked desert toward his destination. Even from this distance, the small town of River, Texas, looked more dead than alive—a collection of rotting wood buildings sprawled along the orange horizon like the half-buried bones of some great beast.

He nudged his cyber-brute from a walk into an easy trot along the cracked asphalt of the old highway, curving around gnarled mesquite trees as he drew closer. Once he moved into the edge of town, Dust could see that at least some of the rumors were true. There was a powerful spiritual pestilence infecting this place and its symptoms were played out in the buildings' weathered wood and its inhabitants' worn expressions.

Most of the buildings looked at least a hundred years old with the newest construction having been done during the last oil boom some fifty years ago. Much of the original brick buildings were crumbling. Repairs had been done with weathered boards and cheap stucco. Dust took in the scene with wary eyes. He wasn't exactly eager to get down to the unpleasant business at hand, but it would be better to get it over with than to stall and risk the deaths of even more people.

Dust could tell by the boarded up buildings on Main Street that the town, like the land at large, had seen more prosperous days. He had seen the dried up creek bed meandering past the city's rotting walls on his ride in, its water long lost to the blistered sky and overzealous farmers and ranchers. What sustained the town now must be the bottom residue of Ogallala Aquifer groundwater and the last squirts of black gold dredged up by a few of the ancient oil pumpjacks still dotting the West Texas desert.

"Mister, come see my girls," a woman called to him from the doorway of the nearest building. The place sported newer paint than its neighbors and its large sign displayed the phrase: "The Doll House – Adult Pleasures for All" in garish red-and-gold lettering. Her coy smile revealed twin rows of brown teeth. "Every one of them is clean and good-spirited. First time is half-price. What's your pleasure?"

Dust shook his head at her. He rode past the brothel and on along the quiet dirt road toward the peeling white steeple of the church. His sweaty mount would need to drink soon or risk injury in this oppressive heat. Hopefully the church still had free water; he knew better than to seek charity from the madam.

The newcomer rounded a corner and spied another person coming down the road from the opposite end. Astride a well-conditioned brute and dressed in commercial-spun clothing, the other seemed out of place in these shabby surroundings. Dust pulled the wide brim of his faded brown hat lower on his head as the stranger approached—semi-silhouetted against the setting sun.

"You're one o' those Soul Wranglers, ain't ya?" the dandy called.

Dust shifted in his saddle, but gave no reply.

"You on the hunt?"

Dust nodded slowly as he took in the other's long trench coat and wiry frame—a perfect combination for hiding guns or even a bomb vest.

"Not to worry, neighbor. I mean ya no harm," the man said, as if reading Dust's thoughts. "Soul Wranglers are scarce 'round these parts, but I figured one'd come soon as word leaked out about our preacher eatin' a bullet from the wrong end of his gun."

Dust frowned. "Suicide?"

"That's what the medical examiner said. Anyway, I've been taking care of the congregation on Sunday mornings until a new preacher arrives. Name's Bill, by the way. Bill Chambers." The stranger held out his grimy hand—an action that revealed a holstered pistol and a badge.

Dust slowly smiled and reached across the space between the two steeds to shake the sheriff's outstretched hand with his own. "Dustin Hitchens. Everybody just calls me Dust. You got a trough somewhere for my mount here?" He patted the sweaty neck of his riding beast. The dun colored cyber-brute whinnied and stamped the street with an impatient hoof, sending curls of fine orange dust into the air.

"Come on over to my place. We'll get yer horse and you watered well."

"Much obliged, Sheriff Chambers." Dust touched the brim of his hat with a calloused brown finger before following the other rider down River's Main Street.

"How long ya been traveling?" Bill asked as he steered his mare toward the left and down a side street.

"About a month," Dust answered, absently rubbing the graying scruff of his chin. He badly needed a bath and a shave. "Made my way down from Old Santa Fe; had to cut a bit east and then swing back west when my quarry flew the coop."

"Performed hex exorcisms along that way, did ya?" Bill asked, glancing at him. Dust's eyes narrowed, but Bill seemed not to notice. "I've heard tell about some strange voodoo magic practiced by the locals up near Amarillo. I figure they get themselves in trouble with demons weekly and with God daily."

Dust pursed his cracked lips and then winced at the pain. He'd have to buy some more petrol jelly from the local dry goods store, if they had any. He watched the back of Bill's head and squinted speculatively. His reception in various settlements was always mixed depending on the education levels of those he met. Most of the common folk took it for granted that he was some strange mix of priest, marshal, and mercenary. More learned persons knew better and gave him a wide berth accordingly. Consequently, Bill's curious friendliness puzzled and unnerved him. Was the sheriff a threat?

Despite the pain, Dust twisted his mouth into a pleasant smile as they dismounted near the hitching post and water trough at the side of the sheriff's house. "So I noticed the brothel on my way in."

"Oh, Madam LaHayne's place." Bill laughed. "Yeah, it's pretty hard not to notice it."

"How long's it been here?"

"Longer than me. Why? You interested in some company?"

"Hardly. It's just that I can tell a town's in bad shape spiritually when the building with the newest paint is the whorehouse and not the church."

Bill grimaced. "I don't know about all that. I've never actually had to worry about investigating or trying to shut LaHayne's place down. There's never been a domestic violence charge or anything in the place. It's clean as a whistle. Truth be told though, even if I could close 'em, the whole town would probably riot when I did. LaHayne's establishment brings in some of the best tax revenue of any business in the entire city."

"I bet it does." Dust patted his mount's neck at it finished drinking. "So, Bill, did you grow up here?"

The sheriff brightened at the change in subject. "Naw. I was born and raised in San Antonio, a fair 400 miles east of here. The wife and I moved out here several years back when oil was still plentiful and the town was still green. O' course, green is a bit of a relative term in these parts." He flashed his yellow teeth in a crooked grin. "Anyway come on in to the house, won't ya'? We'll talk a spell more. Emma will have supper cookin' right about now and she always makes extras."

"That's mighty kind of you, Bill, but I ought to see about getting a room for the night, pickin' up some supplies, and scouting the town a bit more."

Bill frowned as he held his mare's reins. "How long you plannin' on staying?"

Dust squinted and scratched the stubble on his chin. "A week or four. It depends on how long it takes me to track down and undermine my quarry." He gave the sheriff a thin smile. "Given the state of things, I've got a strong suspicion it's here."

Bill gulped, but covered his sudden nervousness with a good-natured grin. "The only place with overnight accommodations in this town is the brothel and I get the feeling that you'd rather not to stay there. How 'bout bunking in with Emma and me? With the youngin gone, we've got plenty of room here. Tomorrow I'll show you 'round the town and get you set with the right people."

Dust frowned. Bill's hospitality seemed genuine, but it didn't feel right—none of it. The Soul Wrangler could feel the walls of his enemy's trap slowly closing in around him, but he couldn't tell where they were coming from. "Again that's awfully kind of you, but I couldn't possibly intrude on you like this—"

"Nonsense! It's our pleasure!" Bill wrapped a lanky arm around him and led Dust and his mount to the corral so that both men could unsaddle their steeds.

***

Supper, as it turned out, was a chicken stew made with corn, beans, and peppers served in chipped bowls by a quiet woman whose face was as delicate as her calloused hands. Dust watched her and Bill while he ate, taking in their shared glances between bites of stew or corn tortilla. He asked about affairs in town. Was there still a working dry goods store or livery stable in the place? What were most people's livelihoods around here? Did the town have a practicing doctor or just a nurse or midwife to tend the sick?

Throughout it all, Bill kept up a lively conversation while Emma remained silent and stolid. Only once did she speak and that was only after the supper dishes were cleared and the men had retired to the back porch for after-supper drinks.

"So, Dust, do you drink?" Bill asked.

The Soul Wrangler shook his head. "Not much now. Maybe an occasional beer when the mood hits me. I don't drink when I'm working though."

Bill laughed. "Well, it's a good thing you're not working now then, isn't it?"

When the Soul Wrangler smiled, Bill told Emma to bring out some tea and then took the liberty of adding a good draught of his own brewed whiskey to the pot. The dark liquor-laced concoction was pleasing, but strong on the tongue. Dust took careful sips of his cup, always measuring Bill's intake and sipping his cup after the other man did. The Wrangler surreptitiously spit his own drink into an empty canteen so that he stayed sober even when his host became rip-roaring drunk.

While he sang songs in the same off-key slur as Bill, Dust's eyes were too keen to fool Emma. She caught him spitting back into his canteen on the back porch just after Bill had gone to use the toilet closet on the side of the house.

"Help me," she whispered, clutching his arm. "He becomes a monster when he's drunk."

That got Dust's attention. "Is or becomes one?"

"*Becomes*," she said, her eyes haunted.

Dust coughed and spewed the rest of the tea over the porch railing. It landed on one of the scraggly bushes and instantly discolored one of the roses. "Dear God in Heaven, what have I been drinking!"

"The whiskey-tea's laced with ghost salts and peyote by his doing, nightshade by mine. I've been trying to kill him, but everything I try only makes him stronger. It's not natural. None of it! I spared the poison tonight, but his drugs are just as stout as usual."

"You think he's more than just high?"

She nodded. "He's possessed."

"How long has this been going on?"

"Two years."

Dust could hear scratching and low snarling coming from the outhouse. He swallowed hard. He'd been too foolish to recognize his enemy hidden in the sheriff. Now it was too late. The trap had been sprung and he was caught squarely in its jaws. "How bad has the possession become?"

"Four dead so far."

"And no one'll stop him?"

She shook her head. "He's bullet proof."

Dust swore, and then apologized to God and to the woman for his foul mouth.

"I don't blame you, if you run. You came here with no back-up."

"The Good Lord is my backup, Emma. Besides if I run, it'll just chase me until I tire and destroy me alone in the desert. With me gone, who knows how long it'll be before another Wrangler can come to your aid."

She nodded wearily and then thrust a small red pill into his hand. "I know you made certain that your tea was weaker, but even so this will purge you of whatever's still in your system."

"Much obliged. How did the manifestation start?" Dust asked before he downed the pill with a swig of water and then retched into the bushes.

"A New Light missionary came to the house seven years ago on his way to Aransas and dropped off several instructional booklets about communicating with ancestral ghosts and nature spirits," she said as Dust sipped water from his clean canteen to rinse the bile from his teeth. "We'd been warned about that stuff being dangerous, but when our daughter died in a tractor accident, Bill took her death real hard. He'd never been an overly religious person to begin with, but those books became his refuge and I thought that, as much as they seemed to help him, what harm were they really?

"The first manifestations started a couple years after that—first in dreams...visions of men and women of light walking toward him, talking to him, teaching him ceremonies and rituals to call forth certain spirits. Then, when he was awake, he started seeing visions of our daughter wrapped in light, begging him to bring her back into our house. I watched him deteriorate and it scared me. To have him act normal one moment and then hear him talk to our Ashley as if she was in the room with us was too much." Emma shuddered. "That night I—I tried to burn the books...that was the first time he struck me."

The outhouse door banged open as Dust wiped the last of the bile from his lips with a red handkerchief and Emma scurried back into the kitchen.

Bill, or at least what should have been Bill, lurched out of the building. He looked exactly the same as he had before except that his face was contorted into the cruelest leer Dust had ever seen. The voice that issued from his lips was a growl too low for a human. "The prince of this land commands you to leave, man of God. You desecrate this place with your presence."

Dust stepped into the yellow grass beyond the porch and threw down his handkerchief like a bullfighter waving his cape at the Toro. "And he sent you to deal with me, did he?"

The Incarnate drew himself to his full height. Despite not topping Dust's own six-foot height, he seemed to tower over all else anyway. "He did."

Dust met the thing's gaze without flinching. "Name your charge, demon."

"Never."

"In the name of Jesus Christ whom I serve, I order you to name your charge."

Bill's pistol found its way out of its holster and toward Dust's face. His sneer deepened as he cocked back the hammer and chambered a round. "Leave this place or die," he threatened.

Dust met the other's wild gaze and slid his hand over the wide belt buckle above his hips. He rapped its cold metallic surface with his fist and a sound like the sweet hum of a child reverberated in the air around the Soul Wrangler. The thunder of the gunshot overpowered the clear note from the belt buckle just as the bullet met the air mere centimeters in front of the Wrangler's face—and shattered.

The monster stared slack-jawed at the Soul Wrangler a moment before firing off another round. It too fragmented against Dust's humming high-speed projectile shield. The fiend snarled, dropped the gun, and charged—his hands curled into claws. Dust sidestepped the charge and kicked his attacker squarely in the knee. He might as well have booted a brick wall for all the good it did.

The monster snatched the Soul Wrangler's leg and hurled him back. Dust tumbled end over end back onto his feet and yelled, "The power of Christ compels you, demon! Name your charge!"

Bill spat in disgust as he crouched. The black puddle of spit looked more like tar than water. "I will kill you, human!"

"Maybe and maybe not." Dust stared him down and reached for his great-great-grandmother's coiled rosary hidden in a pocket of his duster—his only true weapon against demons and their Incarnates. His rough right hand reverently caressed the stone-carved cross at the end of the beaded loop. "Either way you will name your charge in the name of Jesus Christ, whose death and resurrection have given me dominion over you."

The demon cussed vengefully as Bill's body lunged. Dust leapt to the right and circled around his attacker. "Name it!"

"I am charged by my princes as the keeper of despair," the possessed man screeched before charging again.

Despite feeling light-headed, Dust rolled out of his aggressor's path and grabbed Bill's arm as he moved past. The Soul Wrangler flipped the Incarnate around his own body and dropped him headfirst on the grass. Now it was the Soul Wrangler's turn to growl. "I have been hunting you a long time."

The demon's answering smirk showed uneven on Bill's weathered face as he flipped back to his feet. "And so now that you have found me at last, what shall you do with me?"

Dust's eyes went flat with abhorrence for the spirit that had destroyed so many people including, likely, this current host. "Dispel you."

The fiend threw his host's head back and laughed. Even after all of this time, the sound still made the hair on Dust's neck stand straight out like marching soldiers. The cackle was beyond any that a normal man should be able to produce—a sort of half gurgle and half scream. Dust heard it within his spirit as well as his physical ears and frowned. While haughtiness was the strongest emotion conveyed, it barely concealed the fear and hatred writhing underneath.

"You will fail, human."

"On my own, yes, I will. But I can do all things through my savior, Jesus Christ, who gives me strength."

The Incarnate hissed in defiance at the scripture reference and punched at him. "Kill this host and I will simply take another. Don't you and your pitiful brethren ever tire of tracking me? You cannot kill me, only my host. You cannot kill me, but I can and will kill you."

Dust dodged and returned the strike with one of his own. "My job is not to kill you, only to defeat you. Your possessed victim may kill my body just as I can kill his, but we both know that his soul and mine are just as eternal as yours. If you kill me, what have you gained? Another of God's servants gone to be with his Creator, while you and your fellows still rot either in hell or on earth. Don't you ever want to rejoin the winning side?"

The demon swore at him.

Dust sighed sadly. "As always, pride wins over logic."

When the Incarnate lunged at him again, Dust was ready. He gripped the rosary and struck the Incarnate over the neck and shoulder with its cross as he sidestepped the lunge. "Greater is He that is in me than he that is in the world. In the name of Jesus Christ, demon of despair, come out of Bill now!"

The Incarnate stumbled and fell against the hard-packed dirt, his eyes rolling back into his skull.

"Bill!" Emma screamed from the porch.

"Stay there!" Dust shouted. He made the mistake of taking his eyes off his adversary a moment and, in that split-second, paid the price. Bill's right hand pulled a knife from the sheath at his belt and blindly slashed at Dust's nearest leg. It passed through the shields designed only to deflect much faster moving weapons and found flesh. A half-strangled scream escaped the Wrangler's cracked lips as he fell backwards, clutching his bleeding right shin. The knife had bit all the way to the bone.

"You really think I'd leave him so easily?" the Incarnate said as he drew himself off the dead grass and stared down at Dust.

He pointed the bloody knife at him as Dust crawled away. "He's mine and, now, so are you!"

Dust shook his head and whispered, "No" as his leering attacker stepped toward him.

"Bill, no!" Emma screamed. "Oh, God help us!"

"Shut up, woman, or you'll be next!" the Incarnate yelled without even breaking his stride. "Your last living thought, Wrangler, will be that you should have never come to my town."

As the knife whistled down toward Dust's chest, the Soul Wrangler shielded himself with the hand still holding his rosary and tapped his belt buckle twice with his other hand. A sound like the tolling of a church bell reverberated around them as the knife struck.

When the knife collided with the rosary, it might as well have struck a stone wall. Even the Incarnate's superhuman strength couldn't force the knife any further. Instead it glanced off the beads—narrowly missing Dust's fingers—and twisted out of Bill's grasp. As the bent knife fell harmlessly to the ground, Dust pushed himself to his knees and slammed the cross against Bill's chest. The hulking Incarnate fell backwards against the hard ground, cracking his head on the bottom wooden step of the porch.

"I am the resurrection and the light, says the Lord," Dust whispered through clenched teeth as he held his hand over his ravaged leg to try to slow the bleeding. "He who believes in me shall never die."

"No!" cried the demon.

"Bill, I know you're in there," Dust said as he stared blearily into Bill's eyes. "Pray to God and help me get rid of this monster who has taken over you!"

Bill spit at him as he looped the rosary around the possessed man's head. "He's mine, Wrangler, no one else's!"

"Bill is God's, demon of despair, and by Jesus's sacrifice, he is free of you. Leave him now in Jesus's name!" Dust's vision was swimming. He was on the verge of passing out, but he kept pressing the attack. If he didn't win this battle, they were both dead.

"No! Stop!" Bill screamed in agony.

"In Jesus's name, come out of him! Come out of him now!"

Bill gave one last echoing scream and then went limp. A dark cloud seemed to seep out from under his closed eyelids and dissipate into the night. Dust searched his surroundings with both eyes and soul, but he could no longer feel the dark presence that had haunted him since his arrival in River. He motioned Emma to join them from her perch on the far side of the porch.

"It is done," Dust said wearily to her as she clutched her unconscious husband's head with tears falling from her cheeks.

"Thank you," she whispered.

He tried to reply, but the blackness of unconsciousness swallowed his senses instead.

***

When he came to, Dust was staring groggily at the beige-tiled ceiling of a small room. The pain medication had worn off and he felt the needle-prick sting of stitches in his leg every time he moved. He smelled the sharp scent of the clean linen sheets wrapped around his limp body and saw Emma dosing in a chair beside his bed.

"Where am I?" he asked, rousing her.

Her chin came up with a jerk as she looked around startled. When she saw him awake, she smiled. "How do you feel?"

"Well enough. How's Bill faring?"

"He's fine—better than fine, he's back to normal…but he's in jail."

Dust stared at Emma a moment. "I'm sorry."

She nodded. "It can't be helped. I couldn't stitch up your leg myself, so Doc Miller had to be called. Once he got involved, he started asking questions, which meant that Phil had to be called—"

"Phil?"

"Oh, yeah, Phil is Sheriff Deputy Larson's first name. Anyway, once he found out what I knew about the fight and about Pastor Stackhouse's death, Bill went straight to jail and Judge Fuentez set bail at 500,000 bucks. The only reason I'm not in there with him right now is that I agreed to testify in court. Once you're up to it, Judge Fuentez wants you to testify as well."

Dust winced. It had been a long time since he had testified in court as a Soul Wrangler. His ability to sway the jury on a murderer's innocence would be a long shot at best, but he could at least try. "I'll be glad to do that, Emma." He winced again. "Once

I'm healed."

"Thank you," Emma whispered. She looked down at her hands for a minute. "You should know I burned the New Light books."

"All of them?"

"All of them that I could find. I think there are several more around town, but all of Bill's are destroyed at least."

Dust closed his eyes. "Thank you."

"Dust, you might make an announcement. You know, at church? Tell all of the townsfolk about the dangers of contacting the dead and such. There's been gossip all around town about what happened between you and Bill and a Sunday morning sermon from you could go a long way to dispelling those rumors."

Dust opened his eyes and frowned at her. "Emma, I'm a warrior not a preacher. I wouldn't know the first thing about how to give a sermon."

"Still, there's no one else remotely qualified to spiritually lead this town, Dust. Not a one. Our mayor sent off a letter requesting a new preacher to the Good Shepherd's Conference a few days after Pastor Stackhouse died. I asked her about it yesterday and she told me that the Conference ministers are not sending a new preacher because of the lack of church attendance." She rubbed a weary hand over her eyes and sighed. "Some of us were hoping you'd stay. Now I'm begging you."

Dust grimaced. "Emma, it's not that simple. I'm a drifter; that's the life of a Wrangler. I have to go where my quarry goes. I don't just get to decide whether I stay in a place or when and if I settle down for good. That's the Good Lord's call, not mine."

"The God I know protects his own, Mr. Hitchens. He provides for our needs and a lot of our wants. Tell me that ain't so."

Dust grudgingly nodded. "It's so."

"He knew we needed a warrior to help protect us and so he sent you. He also knows we need a leader to help guide us. I think that's also you."

Dust sighed. Something in her words resonated deep inside him. He stared past her and out of the window. The first rays of sunlight were dispelling the early morning gloom and illuminating the dilapidated houses situated across the street from the clinic. Dust knew that there would be a lot of work ahead of him if this town was to have any hope of spiritual and physical renewal. He'd kicked one demon out certainly, but they nested like rats in the souls of men—overthrow one and a hundred more would try to take its place. Was it really worth the fight?

Dust closed his eyes and prayed silently, *Lord, what do you want me to do?*

It's alright, Dust, a quiet but powerful voice answered within his soul. Dust felt a peace beyond all comprehension overwhelm his thoughts. *This is what I want of you. Emma has been on her knees day and night before me and I have listened. Stay in River. Help the people here. I'll show you what to do.*

"Dust?"

Dust opened his eyes and looked at Emma.

"Were you praying?" she asked.

Dust slowly nodded.

"What did God say?"

"That I should stay."

"Are you going to?"

He looked out the window again at the work to be done and smiled. "Yes. Yes, I'll stay."

The Soul Wrangler:
A Duel between Good and Evil

Having grown up among the cotton-fields and mesquite thickets of West Texas, I am well acquainted with the spirit of the Old West. However, it was not until I moved to a small town during my late 20s that I discovered how harsh life in the desert can sometimes be.

In many ways, the little town of River is quintessentially West Texan. It's steeped in sage brush, mesquite trees, sand, and wild fires. It's situated in prime drought country and yet its foundation for existence is mainly groundwater-irrigated farming and oil production. River is one of the roughest of all West Texas towns because its people have rarely known any sort of prosperity. Instead they have had to fight simply to survive. If people fight for survival too long, they'll eventually forget how to truly live. Poverty breeds desperation and, if left unchecked, desperation leads to despair. It is against this hopelessness that Dust firmly makes his stand.

As a teenager, I was fascinated by the way in which Frank E. Peretti's fiction was woven around the war between angels and demons. When I read Stephen King's *The Gunslinger* years later, I found myself longing for one of Peretti's preachers to wander into the scene and teach King's gunslinger a thing or two about true good versus evil. My wish finally gave rise to the character of Dust and his journey to help the dry little town of River. By his very presence, Dust makes it clear that the poor and the downtrodden are worth fighting to protect and aid. He has the authority and ability to take a life if needed, but he would rather risk his own life to save someone else's. Isn't that what a hero should be?

My Hero, His Monster

Sometimes I'm a hero;
But mostly I'm a monster.
Sleeping, wheezing, dead inside,
Always guilty of last night.

Apathy is my drug,
Bitterness my pill.
A swig of hatred
Excites me still.

Lay down your poison.
Give over your sin.
Only as you lose control,
Can you truly win.

Why is it so hard for me
To trade this ugly pride
Why do I cling to it
When I'm so dead inside?

Lay down the pride.
Give over the fear.
You can do nothing
Without me near.

Please help me! I'm falling!
I can't crawl this path alone!
I'm here beside you as always.

Come, let me lead you home.

I scream at the darkness
Be gone, my venom lover,
Awake, Alive I follow Christ
The risen God; my loving savior.

What Tendrils Echo

A surge of pain jolted me awake. My bleary eyes snapped open to see a black jaguar's half-open jaws inches from my face. I tried to scream, but only managed a wheezing cough as the predator's hot breath overwhelmed my nose and slithered down my throat. The jaguar watched me steadily and then seemed to nod to itself. Before I could even flinch, the beast's massive jaws closed on my head. It bit down on my already bloody skull and held me between its fangs while its hot breath streamed into my lungs. The smell was revolting and yet addicting—like I was breathing in pure adrenaline through a moldy sponge. I finally found my voice and screamed. The jaguar jerked back and then growled at me, as if annoyed by my fear. He—I could now clearly see that it was a he—flicked his tail back and forth like my house cat does when she feels smug about something. Then he turned and vanished into the jungle's undergrowth.

I sat paralyzed with my back against a large boulder for several minutes. With nowhere to run and no one to help, I was sure he would return and finish me off. I looked around the jungle floor through tear-streaked eyes, trying to make out any new danger. Nothing moved among the shadows, not even an ant. I listened intently for the faintest sound and heard nothing. How weird. The jungle was always noisy. Day or night, rain or shine, the world was always filled with some sort of cacophony. Yet here in the clearing where I lay there was only silence until…

My stomach roared rather than gurgled. The unexpected noise made me jump to my feet in terror. At least that is what I tried to do. My legs seemed to be asleep because I felt nothing solid under me when I landed. The shock of that lack of sensation caused me to tumble backwards into a tree root the size of my chest. The collision between my skull and hard wood should have sent me cursing or wincing or at least something other than a mere "Huh." Why was I numb from head to toe? What was going on here?

I reached up and felt the gooey wetness of blood coating my hair. As I pulled the hand away from my scalp and examined it, I also noticed a kind of greenish puss-like sap clinging to the dark red smeared on my palm. The mix of sweet and metallic scents made me want to vomit. Instead my stomach just growled all the louder. I had to find safety and food fast.

I looked around my oddly quiet surroundings once more. Where was I? I couldn't remember anything past the unearthing of the Olmec chieftain's tomb's entrance last night after supper. All of the members of our archeology team had been so excited. Was it last night or the night before? Obviously, I had slept since then, but I couldn't remember going back to my tent to do so. I'd never be stupid enough to wander off alone in the rainforest, so perhaps the jaguar pulled me out of my tent and off into the jungle. Had he? I couldn't remember.

"Come on, Jacqueline. Think!" I whispered to myself, but my skull's pounding prevented anything more than the most basic instincts to surface. I wiped the sticky substance off my hand with a handful of leaves, tore off a piece of my T-shirt, and wound the rag around my bleeding head.

I frowned at my wayward legs. The tanned skin protruding from my hiking boots was peppered with cuts from yesterday's excursion to the temple dig site. My skin should be covered with insects and feel on fire, but instead it was just numb with cold. Still frowning, I tried to stand once more. This time balance won out long enough for me to find a fallen branch from a nearby tree and use it as a decent walking cane.

The snap of a nearby twig caught my attention. The jaguar must be back. Well, at least I had a weapon now. If I was going to die, I was going to go out swinging. I braced myself against the closest tree and waited for the jaguar to pounce.

"Jacky, where are you?"

"Edgar?" I half-shouted in surprise.

"Ja-a-a-a-a-cky!"

His calls were closely followed by the crunch of more undergrowth as my rescuers hacked their way into the clearing. My closest friend and archeology colleague Nikki Alvarez was the first to get to me. "Jac! Oh, thank God! Are you okay? You look awful! What happened to your head?"

"A jaguar…tried to maul me," I said as I collapsed in her arms.

"We have to get her back to camp now!" I heard Delores say. I tried to nod in agreement with her, but spots were now floating before my eyes and then my mind went dark.

***

Apparently I made it back to camp sandwiched between Nikki and our resident botanist Edgar Olson with Delores Padilla, our expert anthropologist, leading the way. By the time we made the two-mile journey back to our camp's hospital tent, I had regained some consciousness. I was vaguely happy to see that my limbs had regained most of their normal function. I was still numb and cold, but could feel some warmth whenever my body came in contact with something substantial. Our expedition's physician had been stricken with dengue fever so Delores looked me over once we arrived back at camp.

"It must be handy to have some E.M.T. training," I mumbled as she held the cold chestpiece of her stethoscope to my chest and back.

"Breathe a little deeper for me…that's it. Some days, although I wish the doc were here. I am woefully unprepared for anything beyond the basics." She tested my reflexes and then shook her head. "You're all messed up."

"Thanks," I said sarcastically.

"Between Dr. Carson being so sick, you being missing for three days, and those two dead grave robbers Edgar and I found last night, this week has become everyone's worst nightmare."

"Grave robbers?"

She nodded. "We were returning to camp just before twilight along the San Pedro Trail after looking for you. We came across the two corpses in a clearing roughly a half-mile from where we found you today. I doubt they had been dead for more than a few hours, but the flies were already buzzing. Both men's skulls had been cracked open and the brains had been eaten as had the shoulder meat and part of the lung tissue. It was quite gruesome. Nastiest mauling I've ever seen."

My mind flashed a scene of two large men lying on the ground near a stream with their skulls half-crushed and half of their brains scattered among the leaves. I frowned in consternation. Had I seen them?

"I think I know the spot," I said, while still wondering if it was my memory or my imagination that had just surfaced.

Delores nodded again. "We've all been through there a dozen times, so it wouldn't surprise me."

"You don't think they were after the chieftain's tomb, do you?"

"Why else would they be in this part of the jungle? Besides, they had all the usual equipment with them."

My stomach rolled. "Another jaguar attack?"

"Probably, although the mauling pattern is a bit unusual for that type of big cat."

"So was mine."

She nodded. "Anyway, you're malnourished, dehydrated, and I've never seen a worse bunch of reflexes in my life."

I smirked. I had never been the most athletic of people and told her so.

"You likely suffered a minor concussion when the beast bit you. Even so there's no serious infection to the wounds, even as deep as they are. Frankly, Jac, you're lucky to be alive. If the cat had squeezed any harder he'd have crushed your skull and we'd be carving your headstone right now."

My head was pounding and my stomach lurched. "I felt like I had already died before the jaguar found me. I mean I was numb all over and my head was already gashed open where he bit me just before you came. I think he bit me twice."

Delores pursed her lips and frowned. "Do you realize how weird that sounds? Predators just don't behave like that."

"I know it sounds crazy."

"As it is, you're in no condition to leave here right now. You should regain motor function as time goes on, but I still need to keep an eye on you just in case. Understand me?"

I nodded my head and then winced. Without another word, Delores set to work dressing my head and leg wounds. With her help, I hobbled off the exam table and over to a corner cot. She then handed me a large vial of acetaminophen tablets and a small vial of neomycin sulfate tablets. "These are for your aching head.

Don't take more than one of each every six hours. Do not take either pill without food and water. Oh, and absolutely no alcohol and no work until I say otherwise. Okay?

"I promise."

"I've got to check on the dig. Will you be okay while I'm gone?"

"Yeah, I'll be fine."

She nodded. "You just rest for a while, okay? I'll be back to see to you in a bit."

"Thanks, Delores," I said. I sank into the white of the pillow as she tucked the bed sheet up under my chin. She patted me tenderly on the shoulder. I think I found sleep before she had even secured the mosquito netting around my cot.

***

At some point that night, the dark jaguar visited me in my dreams. I found him sitting stone still upon the half-excavated Olmec burial mound with his massive paws resting upon the unusual obsidian archway entrance that my archeology team had unearthed four days ago. The jaguar himself was crowned with the same circlet that was depicted on the stone carvings of the ancient chieftain and bore a pair of wings that reminded me of clouds and stars. I swear the crown's jade-eyed serpents actually writhed against the gilded facets holding them. Behind him the bone-white barked species of trees that Edgar had yet to identify swayed softly in the breeze that wafted over the tomb. I watched them for a while, entranced by their branches' subtle rhythm.

The powerful cat then stood and launched himself at me through the tomb's archway. As he did so, his body became translucent and then flowed through the center hieroglyph of the arch. When he reemerged, his outstretched claws were like sharpened stingray tails. They melted through my body as he touched me.

The scene dissolved into another. The crowned jaguar was calmly crouched amidst the carnage that Delores had described to me earlier. He was licking bright blood from his dark claws and then growled at me. Then he stood on all fours, stretched out his front paws into a strange kind of bow, and stalked into the shadows—leaving me alone to stare at the grave robbers' mauled corpses.

***

"Well, you're showing excellent improvement," Delores said as she examined me.

I had spent three days in the hospital tent with nothing but weird dreams and angry mosquitoes buzzing outside my cot's mesh canopy for company. I was itching to get back to the excavation site, especially since Nikki and the others had already entered the Olmec chieftain's burial chamber. The team's preliminary examinations revealed carvings never before seen associated with an Olmec burial site and I was dying to get a look at them.

"I see no reason not to let you out today," Delores continued, "provided you keep under shade, continue to drink plenty of fluids, and stay sitting as much as possible."

I rolled my eyes. "Delores, I have twenty people to manage. You don't really expect me—"

"Correction, Jac, you have nineteen people to manage."

I froze. "What?"

"We found Josiah's bloody clothes and a piece of scalp last night. I assume he was mauled and carried off by our neighborhood cat, but we haven't found the rest of him to confirm that yet."

I cursed in English, Spanish, and ancient Nahuatl. "Why didn't someone tell me sooner?"

Dolores cocked an eyebrow. "What good would it have done besides give you a heart attack? You couldn't do anything in your present condition anyway."

"I swear sometimes I think this expedition is cursed," Nikki added as she entered the hospital tent.

My temporary medic's eyes narrowed. "Wouldn't be the first time or so I've heard."

I smiled at Nikki and then turned back to Delores. "You really think it's the same beast that attacked me?"

Delores nodded. "We found skull fragments along with the scalp piece. This suggests the same style of mauling that we found from the first two and you." She cleared her throat, obviously uncomfortable. "If all three bodies had each of their skulls cracked open along with the lungs, heart, or shoulders consumed first, then we're definitely dealing with a jaguar. The weird thing about the first two victims is that the brains were also completely consumed. Doctor Weatherly says that is unusual for a jaguar, but then so is a jaguar hunting humans in the first place…at least in these parts."

I rubbed my forehead vigorously and then stood up from the clinic bench. "Nikki, have everyone move their tents closer to the grave site. I want as much open space between us and the jungle's tree line as possible. Put up some thorn fences as high as you can get them along the camp's outside perimeter. Keep a goat tethered far outside the fence as a prize for the beast. Build watch fires too. Pull as many people off the dig as you need to get the job done. And find out from the Belize authorities what we need to do to legally kill a man-eater if it comes to that. I'll not lose another person to this beast."

Nikki gave a mock salute and flipped aside the white canvas flap. "I'm glad you're feeling better," she said seriously and then was gone.

Delores watched her leave and then turned back to me. "You know, she's been praying constantly for you. It's been rare these days to see her without her rosary in-hand."

I sighed. "At this point, I'll take whatever help I can get."

The atheist smirked. "Even imagined?"

I thought about the nightmares I'd been having ever since my rescue. My stomach flipped when I remembered how real the brain matter had felt when I had held it in my dreams. Should I tell Delores about them? I glanced sideways at her and decided against the admission. I needed a psychiatrist for this problem, not a medic.

I forced a laugh and said, "Even imagined."

***

"I can't believe this," Nikki said for the third time this morning. "I can't believe we've found all of this!"

I stood beside her and stared in awe at the room around us as our colleagues kept busy cutting and brushing earth and roots away from the two colossal stone heads guarding the entrance to the chieftain's burial chamber. They had been half hidden in the walls by soil and entwined roots until our team managed to knock down the partition hiding them. The basalt heads were perfect and whole, not one inch of their magnificent facades showing any signs of mutilation!

The burial mound itself was divided into two large rooms—the king's burial chamber and the antechamber where we were currently working. The two colossal stone heads in perfect condition along with the archway entrance into the Olmec burial mound made this discovery the first find of its kind in the history of archeology. Not only that, but Edgar's core samples from the trees on top of this particular mound proved that the trees growing on top of this tomb were older than even the ancient relics discovered at San Lorenzo—nearly 4,000 years old.

"This is the find of a lifetime!" I said, barely containing my excitement. The archeology teams before us had never had the time or the chance to unearth even half of the mound's archway entrance and here we stood in full view of King Tenguihala's stone carved sarcophagus.

Nikki nodded and grinned as she began gently sifting through a nearby cache of tablets and scrolls. I stooped to help her deposit the first intact scrolls of Olmec writings that either of us had ever seen into airtight containers.

"I can't wait to see what Dr. Kaufmann has to say about this!" I said as we carefully packed each of the writings away for protection. "These confirm his theory that the language of the Olmecs is a proto-Mixe-Zoquean!"

Nikki scooped up the bundle of hard tube cases and reverently cradled them against her chest. "As long as I live, I don't think anything can top this. We're rewriting history, Jac!"

***

Three days after our discovery of the scrolls, I stood staring up at the archway of King Tenguihala's burial mound in the waning daylight with a wad of Dr. Kaufmann's notes crumpled in my hand and a thundercloud of an expression adorning my haggard face. What did these stupid carvings mean? I was sure that I had seen a translation of them somewhere before, but I had yet to find it anywhere in anyone's notes. Over and over again, I saw depictions of the sacred jaguar among the carvings, but I did not understand the context.

The archway's first carving showed King Tenguihala, the eternal jaguar king, being laid to rest in his chamber after a cleansing and desiccation ceremony. Yet no records that I knew of had ever described this particular type of mummification used on any Olmec, much less one of their chieftains. Archeologists had yet to even discover an intact Olmec body until we found the two mummified attendants inside the burial chamber with the king last week. We still had to figure out a safe way to move them from the site to a sterile lab for further examination, but Delores was determined that we would find one.

I scratched my head and looked at the second carving. My eyes gazed at the sight of jaguar warriors submitting themselves to the king's priests in a bloodletting ritual to purify themselves. This looked more like something I would expect to find at a Mayan site, not an Olmec site.

I sighed in frustration and turned as I heard Nikki approaching.

"You should not be anywhere near the dig site this late without someone to watch your back, Jac," she said as she stopped beside me. "The jaguar could easily hide in the overgrowth here and attack you without any of us knowing it. We already came close to losing you once and I don't want to do that again. Besides, with only sixteen of us left, the odds are not in your favor anyway."

Seeing the sudden tears in her eyes, I grimaced. "Sorry. I know better. Anyway, what have you found out?"

She cleared her throat. "The government agreed that we face sound threats from both the local wildlife and from antiquities thieves. They have finally given us authorization to move all unearthed artifacts from the excavation site to the U.S. for further analysis. The local activists are of course pitching a fit about this."

I rolled my eyes. "I offered before to work side-by-side with them on this dig and they flat refused. I wished they'd quit whining. We're doing the best we can and we'll get 90 percent of the find back to the Belize authorities once we've finished cataloging it anyway."

Nikki sighed. "Never good enough for that crowd. We've documented the oldest confirmed Olmec site in the world in the middle of Belize and they still treat us like grave robbers."

I shook my head in disgust. "Start making the arrangements to get as much of the archives packed up and out of here as soon as possible. I don't want anyone to have to stay here any longer than absolutely necessary."

"Yes, ma'am," Nikki said. She started back down the trail and then looked back at me. "Jac, you coming?"

I took one last rueful look at the frustrating figures in front of me and then turned to follow her back toward camp and the eventual comfort of my cot.

***

While the others slept within the flimsy tent city, I walked barefoot under the midnight darkness of the trees. I needed to feel the rich earth, the gnarled roots, and the fresh corpses of leaves beneath the toughened skin of my feet. I was getting hungry again, but food must wait until I had dealt with more important matters.

I arrived at the burial mound and passed through its arched entrance without hesitation. There were lamps to light the gravesite's interior, but I did not need their aid to know where I was going. I reached out to caress the nearest tree root that had woven itself into the stone and dirt of the mound to add strength and structure to the space. I could feel the rhythm of life throb within the pale tendril and waited until my heartbeat matched its rhythm. I smiled as I felt the sweet pulse of a different tree migrate through the soles of my feet—its beat also matching my own. Thus attuned to the plants' impulses, I walked forward. I kept my hand outstretched and my fingers brushing the roots of the wall as I stepped down the root and stone stairway into the heart of King Tenguihala's tomb.

Other members of our archeological team had mentioned a growing sense of unease when working at this dig site and, with the recent killings, several now flat refused to go into the king's chamber—claiming it was cursed. I never understood their complaints. If anything I felt more at peace within the walls of this sacred tomb than I had ever felt anywhere in my life. Tonight, in fact, it felt completely like home to me.

I rounded the last corner of the stairwell and stepped into the antechamber where most of King Tenguihala's afterlife possessions were stored. I gazed at the neatly arranged ceremonial jade daggers and the half-rotted quetzal feather headdresses and frowned. Now what was I supposed to do? I knew I had been led to this hallowed place, but why?

A deep voice suddenly resonated inside the roots beneath my

feet and hands. "Jacqueline."

Startled, I looked through the carved archway and into the king's resting chamber beyond it.

"Jacqueline, come to me…"

I could feel the king's voice reverberate again through the roots beneath my touch. My feet walked forward of their own volition. I saw the king's stone sarcophagus and I immediately lowered my eyes out of respect and fear. When I was close enough to touch the king's sacred resting place, I prostrated myself on the root-laced floor before it.

I could feel the pulse of the roots beneath me as they threaded their way between the seal of the sarcophagus and into the king's wrapped body. Somehow I felt interconnected to the trees as their roots steadily fed nutrients into Tenguihala's once-desiccated flesh. I could feel his muscles rebuilding, his organs reforming, and his mind reawakening. I smiled as the trees' tendrils filled my mind with the echoes of his spirit's whisperings.

"Yes, My King?" I whispered.

At his prompting, I opened my mind to his hungry presence and used connection to the roots to nourish him with all the knowledge I had gleaned from my recent feedings. As the last of the memories escaped my mind into his, my stomach roared awake with renewed hunger.

You have done well for me, Jacqueline. You have helped to nurture me in my weakened state through your contributions.

"Thank you, My King!" I whispered.

But I need more, Jacqueline.

"Sire?"

I need more nourishment. You and Cactli are moving too slowly, Jacqueline. If I am to arise and fulfill my Millennial Reign as Final Keeper of this world, I must have more.

"How much more, My King?"

All.

"All?"

All of your companions.

I frowned. So this was why my own hunger was accelerating. "Very well, I will gather them, My King."

Good, now go and finish your duties tonight before the others discover you.

I stood, bowed, and regretfully left the king's revered presence. I walked out into the night—silent as a shadow—and stole back toward camp. I saw twin orange lights glowing seemingly in midair just beyond one of the outermost tents. Delores and Lucas were having a smoke while they watched the camp's perimeter fence for signs of the jaguar or other intruders.

I smiled coldly as I picked up a rock. I snuck up behind Lucas and dropped him with a solid blow to the head. Before Delores could even cry out, I had her head in my arms. I licked my lips as I felt the tree's strength pulse through my limbs. One quick twist of her neck and she was dead before her head found the ground. It was not safe to feast here so I dragged my two former colleagues to the back of the overgrowth around the burial mound to ensure some privacy—taking care to make it look like my jaguar friend had actually done the mauling.

My fingernails grew into stingray-like claws as I raked the scalp from their heads. Frantically I cracked open the skulls to get at the brains inside. I glutted myself on the sweet stuff until there was none left. I then dug a shallow grave in the mound with my claws and pushed their bodies against the exposed roots to let the trees do their work. When the trees were done pulling the nutrients from Delores and Lucas' bodies and feeding them to My King, the two archeologists would be just another pile of bones hidden in the hillside.

The sound of a soft thump caught my attention and I turned to see Cactli watching me from his perch atop the burial mound. I grinned up at the were-jaguar and whispered, "Don't worry, I saved you the lungs and shoulder meat."

The big cat's eyes glinted as he sprang to my side and began to wrestle his meal away from the insistent tree roots.

"Have you decided which form you will take, young one?" he asked me in between bites.

I nodded. "I enjoy the hunt so much, but the chorus of the tendrils' echoes is so scintillating...I can't imagine not being one of the trees."

Cactli's fangs flashed as he gave a low growl. "It has been many years since I have had a companion and you have learned my lessons well. It is sad that you will not join my hunt after all of this, but even so you will make an excellent addition to the Guardian Chorus."

I was honored by the compliment and told him so.

"We'll see if the master honors your request. You must please him well to earn your place either as one of the sacred undead trees or as a jaguar warrior like me. Now off with you, young one. You are in need of rest."

I bowed toward him and then crept back toward my tent, my stomach full and my mind bursting with the new knowledge gleaned from my former colleagues.

***

I bolted upright with sweat dripping down my back and my hair matted to my neck. What had I just dreamed? I frantically pushed the wet locks away from my skin and looked around the dark tent. I remembered fragments of scenes: seeing the inside of King Tenguihala's tomb, talking to trees, running around barefoot, and having black claws sprouting from my fingertips. But none of it made any sense. One thing I did remember clearly was the incredible power that I had wielded in the dream. I had more strength than any person should be able to hold, let alone a five-foot-four-inch woman. Even now I remembered it and I liked it. Here in the echoes of slumber, I could still feel its intoxicating pull and I wanted more. I shuddered—whether from pleasure or revulsion, I did not know—and stared across the tent at Nikki. She shifted uneasily in her sleep and then opened her eyes.

"Hey, you okay?" she asked when she saw me sitting up on my cot.

I shook my head. "Nightmare."

"You want to talk about it?" she asked through a yawn.

"No. I can't even remember all of it anyway."

"You sure?"

I nodded.

"Okay, night," she said and lay back down. She was asleep before her head hit the pillow. I, meanwhile, spent the rest of the night shivering on my cot despite the night's warmth, trying to remember the rest of my nightmare, and dreading what might happen if I did.

I had almost managed to make it back to sleep when dawn's first light brought the sound of running feet. Nikki and I both sat up as Edgar burst into our tent.

"Jacky, you'd better come quick!"

"Edgar, what's wrong?" Nikki asked.

The botanist stared at me a moment before answering. I could see from his blotchy face that he'd been crying. Whatever his message was, it was bad. "What is it, Edgar?" I asked as gently as I could.

"Delores and Lucas are missing."

***

I gaped at myself in the mirror. I looked half-dead. Granted I was usually as pale as a Caucasian could get, but lately my skin had taken on a gray cast and now my eyes were starting to look jaundiced. To make matters worse, my dark hair had begun to fall out in clumps and cause my scalp to constantly itch. When Dr. Carson had recovered enough to look at me, he feared that I had contracted some form of leprosy and made me wear a mask over my mouth and nose as well as long sleeves and gloves in the steaming hot rain forest to help prevent me from possibly infecting himself or the others. Not that I blamed the man for being cautious. After his own battle with dengue fever, he probably should be more than cautious with everyone else's ailments.

Carson had offered to send me back to the states early to see a specialist, but we had only a few days left to finish the dig and I was determined to see things through to the end. After all, as expedition leader, it was my job to try to get as many people out of this hellhole as possible while they were still breathing.

I rubbed my tired eyes to try to keep the tears at bay. The thought of how many we had lost to the jaguar—of how many friends I couldn't even bury because we could never find their bodies—sickened me. Every night I would see fragmented visions of teammates' panicked faces in my dreams only to discover someone else missing the next morning. It was like my dreams were prophesies. Try as I might I couldn't keep the dreams from coming and, truthfully, I wasn't sure that I really wanted them to cease. Now, even in the daylight, I could sometimes catch a whisper or an echo of the power I felt while asleep. If I was close enough to the king's tomb sometimes I could feel a breath of sudden strength course through my veins. What was wrong with me? I cringed and rubbed my balding head. Had Nikki been right? Was this place cursed? Was I cursed?

My stomach grumbled in hunger and, for some reason, the sound suddenly set my teeth on edge. With a sudden scream, I threw the hateful mirror across the tent. It flipped end over end through the moist air and crashed against one of the tent's metal support poles. My life was the mirror: shattering into so many fragments that I didn't know who I was anymore.

"Jac?" Nikki unzipped the tent entrance and poked her head inside. "You okay?"

I turned away from the fractured reflections and shook my head. "Who knows anymore. What's the head count this morning?"

She grimaced. "I really wish you hadn't used that phrase."

I watched her silently and my stomach grumbled again.

"We had twelve at breakfast this morning."

"Thirteen total." I rubbed my balding head again. "Well, at least we didn't lose anyone last night."

She nodded grimly.

"Let's go check on the crew."

I put on gloves, covered my mouth with a new paper mask, fitted my dusty baseball cap over my thinning hair, and marched out of the tent behind Nikki to the king's gravesite. We passed several workers busily boxing up artifacts large and small in shipping crates. The two carved basalt heads, both of which were taller than me, were being loaded by pulley system onto pickup trucks for shipment ahead of the rest of the artifacts. I had ordered the king's sarcophagus and the remains of two of his attendants to be shipped later in the week, so they remained undisturbed for now.

Nikki and I jumped over a crate filled with jade jaguar masks and stingray-tail knives and headed farther up the hill to check progress on the heads' transport. We found Dr. Carson snapping orders from outside the main burial chamber to move one of the pristine heads into its shipping crate in the bed of one of the pickups.

"Watch that section! One miscue and it'll crush the cab! Good, now ease it to the right a bit...more...okay, start lowering it."

We watched their progress from the safety of the grave's archway entrance. "Looks like everything is progressing nicely," Nikki said. I barely heard her forced cheerful tone. The hieroglyphs on the archway had once again captured my attention.

I stepped onto the mound and traced ashen fingers over the archway's center carving. None in our camp had been able to interpret it and yet every time I looked at it I knew the glyphs were somehow familiar. I knew it was important because of its prominent location, but as I traced my fingers over the angles again, I now felt an almost irresistible spiritual connection to it. And power...there was an echo of power like that of the dreams here as well. How strange.

"Jac, what is it?" Nikki asked from behind me.

I ignored her question and moved to touch one of the gnarled trees growing on the roof of this sacred tomb. I gripped an exposed section of root and felt terrible life throbbing beneath its bark. My heart and the base of my skull began to throb in perfect rhythm with the tree's pulse. I felt its life-force coursing down through its roots where they supported the tomb's walls—not just supported, they had become the walls. Somehow that fact was suddenly significant.

"Nikki, how old did you say those core samples were? The ones that Edgar took?"

"He said the oldest trees had over 3,800 rings on them. But that's kind of crazy considering the compact size of these trunks, isn't it? I mean sequoias can live over 3,000 years, but those trees are huge compared to these wimpy things."

"Not necessarily, but if they are that old then they were probably planted just after this tomb was built." I stared at the carving, the life-beat of the interwoven trees feeling like my own. A single tree trunk ring was made in a year. Thick rings equaled bountiful years while thin rings meant lean years. The blood in my veins felt thick and sluggish and yet my heart was racing.

"I have to see those samples!"

I was running back to the encampment before Nikki could even yell at me to wait. I raced to Edgar's lab tent and just about knocked him over as I threw the flap aside.

"Jacky, what the devil?"

"The tomb's trees' core samples, Edgar, I need to see them. I want the oldest two, two of middle-age, and the youngest two samples side-by-side on the workbench."

The lanky botanist just stared at me. I don't think he had ever seen me this flustered or bossy, but I didn't care. "Now, Edgar!"

"Okay, okay, I'm on it." He pulled the samples out of their cylindrical casings and laid them out on the long workbench for me to see just as Nikki swept aside the tent flap and collapsed panting into a chair.

"Nikki, get me the dates of the failed expeditions to this site."

"Jac, what are you trying to—?"

"Just do it!"

Without another word, Nikki disappeared out of the tent entrance and returned minutes later toting her laptop. She plugged it into the electrical outlet strip attached to the field lab's generator and flipped open the screen. Blank black turned to a desktop portrait of Nikki's two kids and late husband as the computer booted up.

"Hang on, let me find it," Nikki said as she began scrolling through the files listed in her documents folder.

"Here it is." She clicked the cursor on a .pdf document entitled "Ancient Wonders of Belize: Expedition I Itinerary." A page popped up with a grainy photo of Dr. Phillip Palmer and 20-odd smiling team members embedded under the large "Ancient Wonders" title. Below the picture, plain block text read: "March 4-May 13, 2006" followed by scheduled meeting times, work visa information, and other miscellaneous information.

Nikki sighed heavily and shook her head. "Not a single one of them survived the guerrilla attacks."

Edgar scuffed his tennis shoes. "They knew the risks just as we do, but it doesn't make it any better. The jaguar attacks don't make me breathe any easier either."

I said nothing, but instead stared back and forth between the core samples and the expedition date. "Nikki, what were the dates for the second expedition?"

She pulled up the second expedition's itinerary. Was it just me, or did the people in this group photo look a little less enthusiastic about their chosen destination?

"March 8th through May 10th of 2008."

I counted the rings backwards, marking each dark mark on the core stick with a pencil. The youngest saplings at the dig site had been alive for about four years and yet their birth ring was much wider than it should have been. I penciled their birth in 2008 on the corresponding rings of the other samples. The year of 2008 showed to be a good one. All of the sample trees showed wide rings indicating unusually high nutrient intake. "Were there any site trees born in 2006?"

Edgar frowned and double-checked the labels on the storage

cylinders. "Yes. Why? Do you need them?"

I shook my head and made note of 2006 on the older samples. "Do we know of any other attempt at an archeological dig in this area prior to 2006?"

"There might have been one in the 1980s."

I counted the cores back to the 80s and found one wide ring in 1987. Before that, the rings mostly stayed thin until much closer to the center of each trunk.

"Look at this!" I said "The first five hundred years of the ancient trees' existence shows them taking in a steady stream of nutrients like clockwork."

"So."

"So, then all of a sudden the rings stay thin for well over 3,000 years until a spike of nutrients as well as new trees start to grow in the 1980s and then again in 2006 and 2008."

Edgar squinted at the rings. "This does not fit with any normal tree growth I've ever seen. It doesn't follow rain and weather patterns of any sort. There aren't even any markings of obvious fire damage."

I nodded vigorously.

Nikki stared at me in confusion. "Jac, what are you getting at?"

I looked at her open-mouthed for a long moment, trying to articulate a conclusion that I felt in my bones, but could not yet explain. Finally I shut my mouth and hurried out of the tent with both Edgar and Nikki right on my heels. I did not stop until I stood just in front of the burial mound entrance once again. My eyes followed the line of hieroglyphs around the archway and then came to rest on the center carving once again. Finally I understood what I was seeing.

"They're Guardians," I said, with awe quieting my voice.

"What?"

"The trees. They're Guardians of the tomb and its king, who is not Olmec by the way. I think he actually predates them by a few centuries."

"Jac, have you completely lost it?"

"Not according to this" —my hand waved at the archway. "Nikki, look at the glyphs." I said, tapping the carvings with a twig I'd just picked up. "The first is of the king being laid to rest in his eternal chamber after a cleansing and desiccation ceremony."

"Yeah, okay, so?"

"The second shows his bravest jaguar soldiers submitting themselves to his priests in a bloodletting ritual to purify themselves. The way that this ceremony is conducted is different from everything we know about Olmecan culture, but never mind. I'm going to assume the warriors were also preparing for the afterlife because of the similarities of the two rites. Then look what comes next. This center carving shows a were-jaguar breathing on the warrior's corpses."

"What's your point?" Edgar was frowning at me with his arms crossed on his chest.

"My point is the fourth and fifth carvings," I said as nightmares and memories suddenly began to merge in my mind. "The warriors are first resurrected by the were-jaguar's breath and then they consume the brains and hearts of lesser peoples for a time before their final transformation. See how the fifth carving depicts this human upon the altar over King Tenguihala's grave? Look at how the trees' tendrils are performing the same bloodletting ritual originally undergone by the original warriors. The language glyphs beside the carvings confirm that this burial mound is meant for human sacrifice for the sake of the mummified king!"

"How could you know this?" Nikki's voice was quiet with either awe or fear. I wasn't sure which. "It...it's not obvious to anyone else."

I gazed at the Guardians' branches as they swayed without wind, while my head and heart began throbbing in time with the hypnotic rhythm of their life once again. I placed my hand upon a pulsing root and felt my consciousness meld with the alien awareness under my fingertips. Tendrils of knowledge awakened and I finally felt the full power of eternity blossom inside me.

I felt the echoes of the king's voice in my mind. *Finish your task for me, Jacqueline.*

"Because the king has chosen me to be a Guardian," I whispered as I felt insatiable hunger rising inside me. I could feel my decrepit body begin to change—growing stronger from the trees' gift of nourishment but desperately needing something more.

I turned toward Edgar and Nikki and smiled. They had both backed farther away from me, retreating from the beautiful trees. I ripped off the mask and gloves and started toward them—my arms outstretched and my fingernails thickening into stingray-like claws. My colleagues screamed and ran from me as I felt tendrils sprout out under my ball cap and then felt gray bark envelope every part of my skin.

Our team members shouted in rising panic as I attacked from the front and Cactli appeared snarling from the rear. Together we trapped the last of the king's needed sacrifices near the mound and pushed them ever closer to the Guardians' waiting tendrils. The jaguar lunged toward Nikki and she screamed. She scrambled back out of his range, clutching the gold cross dangling from her delicious throat. I started toward her, my ash-gray toes growing a little longer with each step. I kicked off my splitting shoes to make room for the roots sprouting from the tips of my feet. I was hungry; the Guardians were hungry. They had not consumed flesh or mind in two days and they craved both from these strange new people. Who knew when more would come to satisfy the bloodletting tradition and add more wisdom to our king?

"I'm sorry," I said, "but I must feed your bodies to the Guardians so they may be strong enough to reawaken Apoxilte Tenguihala for his Millennial Reign. They thrive on your flesh and I on your mind. They must live...I must live."

"Jacky, don't do this!" Edgar pushed Nikki farther behind him and started toward me with his field knife raised.

"I have done my part to prepare for the final transformation. I have fed on the corpses by night. Now, we will feed on the living by day," I said calmly and knocked him aside with twice the strength that I should have had. He fell against the mound and was instantly covered in snaking tree tendrils.

Nikki screamed again and stumbled backwards as I gripped her neck.

"Oh, Jesus!" she cried and wildly shoved her crucifix into my face. At the mention of that horrible name, a blinding shaft of pain cut through the power of the king's and tendrils' echoing voices and I was myself again. In a moment of agonizing recognition, I let go of my best friend and fell to my knees in horror.

"Run, Nikki, run! Tell everyone to flee this place and never ever come back!"

The tendrils' echo again crowded into my thoughts and I felt my individual motivation overridden by the king's insatiable hunger. I tried to grab for Nikki, but she had already pulled out of my reach.

During my hesitation, Dr. Carson shouted, "Stand clear!" and released the straps holding one of the dangling stone heads. It hit the ground just behind the nearest truck bed and began rolling downhill. Cactli tried to escape its onslaught, but it crushed his back paws.

"Cactli!" I screamed and ran to help my battered ally.

As I did so, Nikki jumped in one pickup cab and Dr. Carson in the other.

"Everybody pile on!" Nikki yelled as the trucks' engines roared to life.

A sharp hiss filled my mind and the king's anger flooded my senses. *Do not let them escape!*

I ran toward my prey as the trucks bounced over the dirt road winding through my master's jungle, but they were moving too fast.

Disgraced! the king hissed in my mind as I returned to the mound.

"We have the one," I replied as I reached toward Edgar.

Insufficient nutrients. I need more.

"There is none, My King."

There is you. I will take the full knowledge of the nine you slaughtered and your own knowledge into myself through your sacrifice.

"No!" I screamed.

The tendrils' whispers ceased even as thick roots wrapped around my body. I was yanked into the air and pulled backwards toward Edgar's already emaciated body. I fought the tendrils' hold and screamed again. "I was chosen as one of your Guardians!"

No longer, cursed betrayer! The king hissed in my mind as the Guardians' bark pierced my skin. I was lodged into the side of the hill under the corpse trees beside Delores's cache of bones.

At least, I thought, *I will feel no pain as they consume me.* Then I saw the life leave gentle Edgar's eyes and the king's last word echoed in my mind.

Betrayer.

What Tendrils Echo:
The Siren Song of Power

"What Tendrils Echo" was a very chilling story for me to write. The story itself began after I read a scientific article about a rain forest fungus that attacks the brains of some species of ants and overrides their mental functions so that they purposely sacrifice themselves to help propagate the fungus. The idea of a "zombie ant" so intrigued me that I couldn't help but ask the question: what if a parasitic plant could control human minds the way this fungus controls the brains of ants?

The idea of a plant zombie human was interesting, but I wanted to go deeper with the concept. I have always been an ambitious person. I push to be the absolute best at everything I do, but especially in my creative work. In and of itself, ambition is a healthy thing. But when ambition dips into power lust, it becomes extremely dangerous and corrosive to the human spirit. Therefore I wanted a story that would remind me what some of the consequences might be if a person put her thirst for power and knowledge above the quest for love. I don't mean love in the sense of finding and caring for a spouse. Rather I mean love in the general context of friendship.

How blind with power lust would you have to be in order to betray your closest friends? Is the sacrifice of friendship worth this newfound power? These questions, coupled with the notions of plant zombies and ancient curses, were what drove this story to its inevitable creepy conclusion.

City of Twilight

The setting sun peeked through the gray clouds, illuminating the cracked concrete with its wan light. Darkness would soon overtake the city and once again release the Nightmares, but for now the sunlit ruins were relatively safe.

"I hope so anyway," Carn murmured.

The shaggy black werewolf sat quietly at his post on the grassy hill and surveyed the shattered buildings closest to his forest home. His hazel eyes constantly darted from shadow to lengthening shadow as he searched for movement among the ruined streets while his nose continually sampled the damp air for unnatural odors.

He could still make out the architectural details of the crumbling building nearest to his section of forest—a stone virgin stared at him with blackened eyes as she knelt beneath the remnants of a cracked cross. There was little left of the structure's steep roof and even less of its flower-shaped, stained-glass windows. What had the church looked like when it was whole? How manicured had Carn's forest been when it still acted as the central park to this enormous American metropolis? The Human Plague had reduced the city surrounding Carn's home to a necropolis. Then the subsequent 40 years of Nightmare Wars had twisted it further into a ruin. It was a pity that so much beauty had come to such spoil.

"A pity, but not unexpected. As my father always said, 'Pride goes before destruction.' And the human scientists had more pride than even the worst angels," Carn said and shook his head. "If the fools hadn't tried to kill us off with the Henbane Virus, most of them would still be alive to threaten us today. How ironic."

Carn's tongue lolled out, but his silent laugh quickly faded as a cold tingle suddenly crawled the length of his spine. Frowning, he checked the nearby underground cache of Henbane Catalyst that he and his packmates used to bolster their shape-shifting abilities. Carefully he pulled out the black rubber stopper of one of the glass vials with his fangs and took a small sip before resealing the container. His laugh returned as the warmth of the formula spread out from his stomach to his extremities. He flexed the muscles in his limbs appreciatively as the serum took full effect. He would be ready to shift from a wolf into a human and back again in a few moments' time if the need came.

He took a quick inventory of the full vials as he stashed his brew once again. More than enough to last the month. *Good,* he thought. *We'll not have to run to the Sinai Ruins for more until the next full moon, then.*

And speaking of running...

Carn's ears perked at the sound of fast footfalls. His eyes followed his ears to the corner of a half-shattered apartment complex and spied a frantic human female sprinting across the broken pavement toward the safety of the trees.

Her eyes and voice were filled with terror. "Help me, someone, please!"

The werewolf growled in surprise. He knew of only two human families still living on the outskirts of his forest territory. His pack held protection pacts with both of them, which allowed their members to come to the forest on hunting and bartering trips. This female belonged to neither of those clans. Carn howled a warning to his scattered pack as he ran to intercept the stranger.

A shadow of huge feathered wings swooped in behind her as she reached the tree line near Carn's position. The werewolf dropped into a defensive crouch as the harpy swooped toward the human. The woman screamed as the harpy's razor-edged talons clenched shut—ripping twin shreds down the back of her bloused black shirt. She dove for the ground before the harpy could catch a firm grip on her would-be prey.

While Carn might not entirely trust humans, none of them had ever proven more treacherous than the Greek bird monsters that constantly besieged his forest territory. Their kind had been trouble ever since they migrated off the last functioning trading barge during Carn's father's time as pack leader. The humans, however, had stayed out of the forest—preferring to trade hand-made goods in exchange for some of the pack's food and gathered resources rather than try to take what they needed by force.

The Bernstein Clan is especially useful now that they've learned to make the Henbane Catalyst. Carn frowned. *If this female is somehow related to the Bernsteins and they find out that she died because I did nothing to save her…*

Without another thought, the werewolf leaped to the human's aid—snapping at the harpy before its talons could rake the flesh from the human's head. The harpy screeched at the lunging werewolf while the human backed away from both of them in panic. She suddenly found herself trapped between the werewolf, the harpy, and a stand of trees. With nowhere to run, she crouched against the rough surface of one of their trunks and tried to avoid the harpy's next aerial attack. It was Carn's biting ferocity, however, that became her best defense.

"That's my kill, werewolf!" the harpy called when she finally landed on the branch of a nearby tree to clean her wounds and preen her gray feathers. She looked like an oversized eagle except for her head which was shaped like a human's. Her black lips pulled away from her venomous yellow fangs in a snarl.

Carn howled a second warning and then seamlessly changed his form into that of a dark-skinned human, leaving only the sharp fangs in his mouth unchanged. The girl gave a cry of surprise at his transformation, which then turned into a strange coo of appreciation.

Carn glanced at her and smiled before narrowing his eyes at the harpy. "Since you both have crossed into this forest's territory, you must now deal with my pack's laws. Those laws call for the protection of the innocent and the annihilation of any of the Nightmares or their allies."

"Good, then we're agreed on the matter," the harpy said. "Now hand her over."

Carn bared his fangs. "Any creature seeking to kill a young human female isn't on my list of innocent, harpy."

The bird woman rolled her eyes. "Oh, good. Another male who'll fall to his doom over a pretty face. Look, genius, she's dangerous. Just give her to me before someone gets hurt."

Even with Carn's human form's ability to climb, the harpy

was still well outside of his attack range. While he was alone, he had the advantage and they both knew it. Still Carn snarled. "This forest and everything in it belongs to my pack by right of birth and war. The human—"

"She's not—"

"Silence! The human ran into my territory seeking aid and so she is under my protection against you. If you wish to declare yourself free of my domination and claim her as your own prey, then you must do so by challenge."

"Is that your challenge, pack leader?"

"Take it as you wish, harpy."

The harpy finished picking the debris out of a claw with her poisonous fangs. She then pointed the claw at the human. "That bloodthirsty monster has crossed my flock too many times. She killed my sister and I've sworn to destroy her even if it means my own death."

Carn glanced at the pale human who now sat whimpering with her knees pulled against her chest. The girl looked thin as a reed from malnutrition. She couldn't be older than eighteen. He cautiously sniffed her scent and discovered nothing besides honeysuckle and fresh-tilled earth.

"Oh, yes, truly this is a dangerous creature," the werewolf mocked.

"I'm telling you she killed my sis—"

"Enough of your lies, harpy," Carn growled, suddenly aching for a fight. He flexed his massive muscles, looking every bit as powerful as the American football linebacker from his dead father's pictures. He glowered at the bird-woman between full fangs while calculating the speed and angles of his possible attacks. "Your species has never been friendly to mine, so why should I trust you? The human is under my protection. Care to challenge my authority or the fangs of my pack?" His fingernails thickened into claws once more and his eyes glowed incandescently.

From far off, they heard the eerie howls of Carn's packmates as they raced to their leader's aid. As the harpy hesitated, Carn spoke quietly to the quivering human. "If you wish to stay here in my pack's territory, you may. But be warned, if you choose to stay within the forest, you must become one of us. Otherwise, I cannot guarantee your safety with either my packmates or with the other lesser creatures occupying these woods."

He stared pointedly at the harpy, who clicked her sharp teeth at him. He saw the human nodded her understanding out of the corner of his eye. She did not speak. She was still very pale and her dark eyes carried a haunted gaze. Carn wondered what damage this harpy had already done to her.

"Leave this place!" He roared viciously and sprang at the bird-woman, swinging a clawed hand. The harpy leaped off her perch just before his claws reached her and hissed, her eyes narrowing in defiance.

"You'll regret this, werewolf!" She launched herself higher and soared through the dark cloudy sky back toward the decaying necropolis.

When she had disappeared from his sight, Carn cautiously approached the human—once again catching her sweet aroma of honeysuckle as he moved. "All is well now. She has gone and you are safe with me, I promise."

The female watched him with those captivating dark eyes.

"What is your name?" the werewolf asked gently.

The human hesitated as she looked toward him. "Neme. I am called Neme," she replied as she cautiously edged away from the tree.

Carn looked down at her. She was small, but she carried herself with confidence. Her beautiful dark eyes and hair enthralled him; she would make an excellent member of his pack and perhaps a good mate when she was a little older...if she was willing...

"Do you wish to stay here and learn the ways of my kind?" he asked.

"Yes..." she responded, her dark eyes half-closed, "...I'm hungry."

Carn's smile was one of indulgence. "Don't worry about that. There are plenty of rabbits and deer here. We can go hunting once I have bitten and transformed you. It will hurt a little, but you should be fine within a few hours..."

"Hungry..." she whispered and reached up to encircle his broad shoulders in her arms. The feeling and scent of her so close to him was wonderfully intoxicating. She stood on her tiptoes to close the distance between them and kissed him hard on the mouth. The kiss seemed to last a while before Carn was finally able to pull out of it. Her lips bred incoherence into his thoughts. He backed away from her, shaking his head to clear the sudden cloudiness.

Something is wrong...

He suddenly felt as weak as a newborn pup. The female calmly walked toward him. All traces of her former timidity was now replaced by a haughty leer. She caught him again and kissed him in pure lust before he could resist. The second kiss further clouded his mind and the next moment he found himself on his back against the ground with the female's face hovering above his own.

Carn saw a white glimmer against the night's inky darkness as long fangs grew out of the female's mouth. Her true scent, a putrid reek, finally overwhelmed her pheromone-laced perfume and he suddenly realized she was anything but human.

"Vampire!" he gasped.

Carn tried to pull away from her, realizing in panic that his numb body would no longer respond and that his pack would not reach them in time to stop her from bleeding him to death.

"Now, now, don't be shy; we'll have so much fun together..." the Nightmare whispered gleefully as she straddled his chest to get better access to his neck.

She bent close and ran a sharp tongue over his throat to prepare his skin for her fangs. Her death-bite, however, never touched his neck. Instead she gasped and lurched sideways as a stake tore through her heaving chest. The vampire tried to swipe blood-red claws at her attacker, but the harpy easily dodged the clumsy strike and swooped in to gnaw on the Nightmare's own throat, partially paralyzing it with venom from her own deadly fangs.

The vampire rolled off Carn, clutching at her mangled chest and neck in shock—her corpse twitching in the grass where she fell. The werewolf blinked hard as the fog lifted from his mind. He slowly sat up with a hand pressed against his throbbing temple. He watched silently for a long time as the harpy sat on her former perch, cleaning the vampire's blood off of her ruffled feathers and then spitting out her rancid taste.

He shifted his sight to the Nightmare's now motionless corpse. "She moved in daylight. How could she move in daylight?" he asked in shock.

"She is called Nemesis among the vampires—a very old and powerful creature. Too powerful be bothered by indirect sunlight."

Carn nodded cautiously. "I have heard of her. The humans of ancient Greece used to worship her as a goddess of vengeance and retribution."

The harpy smiled crookedly. "They certainly got the retribution part right. My flock and I had been hunting her for months until she fled to this place. All died trying to destroy her except me."

The scents of the other packmates strengthened as they each drew close. Carn growled low, signaling them to wait, before he turned to look uncertainly at the harpy crouched above him. "Why would you be foolish enough to hunt her in the first place, especially here?"

The female bird-woman gazed at him coldly. "My family's profession is the eradication of Nightmares; we specialize in destroying vampires, succubi, and incubi. Nemesis and her coven made war with us decades ago when they slaughtered the humans under our protection and killed my grandmother for interfering in their feast. She was the first of my family to die by Nemesis's fangs and my sister Kathryn was the last."

Carn stared at the harpy in disbelief. "Nightmares are far more vulnerable when they are feeding. It would have been safer for you to stake her once she had bitten me, but you took the extra risk and saved me instead. Why?"

The harpy continued to clean her wings. "I am tired of seeing death caused by that monster. Besides, she hasn't been able to feed in a fortnight. It made her sloppy." She said it matter-of-factly, but Carn noted the droop in her shoulders as she spoke.

The werewolf's eyes softened as he realized the harpy's sister must have been the Nightmare's last meal. "Where will you go now?"

The harpy shrugged and continued to preen.

Carn sought the eyes of each of his packmates as they encircled the odd pair. Most nodded their furry heads in silent consent and so he turned back to the bird-woman. "You are still in my pack's domain and are therefore subject to our laws, harpy," he said seriously.

Caution suddenly flitted across the harpy's human-like face

as she looked from him to his werewolf allies.

"What is your name?" he asked.

"Elpida," she said slowly.

Carn smiled again, knowing her reputation as an accomplished Nightmare Slayer. "A name meaning 'Hope'. How fitting. Well, Elpida, you certainly have given us some. To show my thanks for saving my life and consequently helping to ensure the survival of my pack, I offer you asylum in our forest for as long as you wish to stay here."

Elpida stared at him in shock before finally stammering, "Really? Do you swear that? On your honor and on the loyalty of your pack?"

Carn nodded. "I swear it, Elpida. And please forgive my earlier rudeness; if I had known…"

"I did try to warn you, but I saw that you were already under her sway."

"And so I was." Carn shook his head and sighed. "That is the first time my keen sense of smell has ever endangered me."

The harpy suddenly smiled. "I think this is the first time a truce has ever been struck between our races, pack leader."

"So it is; may it not be the last. Oh, and call me Carn."

The harpy smiled slyly as she fluttered to the ground and extended her talon to shake his clawed hand. "Short for 'Carnage'?"

The werewolf laughed. "Short for Carnegie, actually. Welcome to my pack."

The werewolves howled in joy as the crescent moon rose high. Once the sentry fires were lit along the boundary line of the forest, Carn ordered the vampire's body to be burned as well so that she could never reanimate and kill again.

As the last of the ancient Nightmare's remains were consumed, Elpida bowed her head. "It's done."

Carn studied Elpida's conflicted continence in the combined firelight and moonlight. Peace between the natural races was often as tenuous as the moon rays, but this pact could prove strong enough to spark a prosperous future for the survivors of humanity's twilight.

Elpida turned to him as he watched her. "Feeling sympathy for me now?"

He shook his head slightly. "Empathy, actually. My father and my brother were killed by Nightmares as well. So, while we might not be of the same race, we still have much in common."

She smiled slightly, but said nothing more. Instead, both of them stared past the boundary fires, waiting to destroy the next Nightmare unfortunate enough to find them before the break of day.

City of Twilight:
The First Short Story

Those who have followed my writing career from its earliest days might be surprised to know that "City of Twilight" not "Sumari's Solitude" was actually the first short story that I ever wrote. Granted, "Sumari's Solitude" was the first of my short stories ever submitted and successfully published, but it was actually the third or fourth short story that I had ever written.

The kernel idea for "City of Twilight" actually came from one of my conversations with an artist at AggieCon in 2006 about the relationships between werewolves, vampires, and humans, in general. The result was a post-apocalyptic story with a decent amount of hope. I love irony so I suppose it should not be surprising that my first story would reflect that.

My Love for Thee

The rains flow with the stream
And sweep into the seas.
Yet none their myriad score
Could define my love for thee.

The sun floods through the breeze
And warms the fruits of trees.
Yet not the sweetest core
Could portray my love for thee.

The hymns of angels speak
And fill the air with peace.
Yet not the gentlest lore
Could express my love for thee.

Not all the earthly lees
Nor even Heaven's streets
Could describe My love for thee
For I love eternally!

Raven's Fall

Raven sat stone still watching light ripple and flow along the banks of darkness. She clutched the cattail reed tightly in one gray talon and pondered the light's myriad weavings through shadow into the world beyond the Falls. Could a world of dawn be so much better than this domain of dusk? The red cattail could give her the answer, but did she dare use it?

"Well, what have you decided?" cried a voice behind her.

Raven's black feathers ruffled in irritation. "That this is some of your usual subversion, Wolf."

The gray canine spirit's tongue lolled out with his yipping laughter. "I cannot hope to trick one so wise as you, Raven."

The great bird spirit said nothing, but continued to stare at the light winding its way out of their world into the world of light.

"I know you tire of this shadow realm as do I, High Spirit. Would it not be a great adventure to see beyond the darkness?"

"Dawn light has no place for us, Wolf. We rule the night as is proper. Only the foolish would wish otherwise."

Wolf nodded. "Oh, indeed. I merely suggested you visit the world of light to better understand the contrasts between black and light. The red cattail will allow you to come back whenever you like."

Raven's eyes narrowed. "How do I know your words are true?"

Wolf's eyes were soft as he replied, "Because you know that I would never wish you harm." She stared at him a long while until he lowered his gaze.

"I have made my decision, then. I will go and see what is to be seen. Will you wait for my return?"

Wolf nodded and stepped back to give Raven proper room for her dive into the river of light. Raven stretched out her lustrous black wings and pumped them hard to hover over the sparkling eddies. She then swooped to grab a surprised Wolf before banking toward the river. Into the rolling light they both plunged. The waves washed away their darkness as they tumbled over the Falls together.

As they rushed into the frothing sea below the Falls, the light branched out in all directions until at last they tumbled in water instead of light. The currents were so tumultuous that Raven lost hold of the red cattail. She tried to swim after it, but her water-logged feathers weighed her down and she began to sink. She swallowed water when a sharp pain lanced through her left wing. Panicked, she tried to strike Wolf as his teeth pierced her flesh.

As Wolf pulled her to shore, Raven screeched, "What have you done? Now I cannot fly!"

"I have done nothing but save you from drowning! It was you who dragged me across the worlds' boundary and then lost the reed!"

"Why did you save me instead of the reed? Neither of us has a way to return to our world now!"

"You are worth more than worlds, even with a broken wing."

Raven began to cry and the tears soaked through her feathers to drip into the sand underneath. The feathers then began to drop into the mud at Raven's feet. It was from this mass of Raven's feathers and sand that a great clam sprang. Wolf broke open the clam to retrieve its pearl, which bubbled with laughter as Wolf held it out to Raven.

As Raven reached to cup the mollusk gem in one featherless wing, her outstretched bones refined into a five-digit hand. Her talons then became feet and the rest of her body became that of Woman.

Wolf yelped both in delight and embarrassment for he had never before seen her featherless form. "Dry your tears and behold this great beauty. Your body now shines as bright as the Light's end held in this world's orb," he said.

Instead, Raven could only stare at her lost plumage and sob all the harder. Wolf sighed and took off his own fur so that he could cover her nakedness. Once the deed was done, Wolf's body became that of Man and he too felt shame at his bareness. Raven blessed the broken clamshell and used both halves to cover Wolf's bare skin. She then planted the blessed meat in the sand along with her discarded feathers and tears.

"Wolf, I will set this gem in the sky opposite the existing light orb as a reminder of what we have lost and what we have gained. I will call the yellow orb Sun. What shall I call the white pearl?"

Wolf gazed at Raven's reflection in the sea gem with utter longing. "Call it moon."

Raven nodded and then threw the laughing pearl into the sky where it remains today. "It is so."

And so the dawn world became one of dark and light with the sun to rule the day and the moon to rule the night. As the moon's first light struck the burial mound of clam meat and feathers, Raven and Wolf heard laughter under the sand. Carefully, Raven delved into the mound only to screech in surprise as she discovered Otter bounding out of the sand toward the water. That first nightfall heard Otter laughing among the waves of the sea, Raven constantly searching and crying for the lost red reed, and Wolf singing longingly about the moon-maker's beauty—just as their animal ancestors do today.

Raven's Fall:
Mythology Takes Flight

My personal library currently consists of more than 500 books and roughly half of these are dubbed my "research books." I have books discussing the workings of siege engines, identifying different types of trees, discussing various religions, documenting numerous scientific disciplines, and introducing various mythological creatures. The genesis of the "Raven's Fall" short story came from reading this last type of research book.

I am a great fan of mythological creatures of all shapes and sizes. And so when I came across a few Native American tales describing the character of Raven, I was instantly intrigued. Throughout these legends, Raven proves time and time again to be a character of inordinate power and great mischievousness. With these traits in mind, I decided to write my own tale about Raven. I wanted to showcase her power, her curiosity, and her foibles. What better way to do this than to introduce her alongside the loyal yet secretive character of Wolf. I think they make a fascinating couple. Don't you?

The Banner Prophesies

Smoke coiled about the battlefield as the unicorn and griffin circled each other. Round and round they paced, testing each other's weaknesses. The unicorn mare's silver hooves flailed against his golden talons and drew scarlet blood. It stained the moorland's dying grasses. Not that the successful attack mattered. The male moved all the faster with the sudden spilling of his blood, his jagged scars stretching over his bulging muscles as he pounced toward her. His body bore more scars than hers, but most of these were shallow and that worried her. The unicorn mare was sleek and smart, but this Sindon beast was proving a more cunning fighter than his predecessors. When she attacked again, he feinted and then snapped back at her with all the ferocity of a true steppe predator.

They kicked and bucked at each other again and again. Her right hoof opened a scarlet gash in his golden chest and his left talon scratched her right cheek. His persistence soon scored a painful gouge even as she bit his feathered neck in return. Her back kick crippled his left wing and his beak snipped off the end of her right ear. Her pained scream echoed off the dark bark of the distant pines even as she tried to spear his left forearm with her spiraled horn. The attack failed and the griffin's reprisal opened a gash in the unicorn's left flank.

She fought on, heedless of the pain, trying to protect her home and her foal from this monster. Like many before him, the griffin of Sindon had tried to expand his territory by conquering hers. The lush forests and verdant fields beholden to the Auleig unicorn would perfectly ornament his vast domain and so the griffin had trekked across his deserts and steppe regions to battle her for dominance. His coming was like the torrent of a firestorm, scorching all life as it swept through the land. The unicorn longed for peace, yet saw none while the griffin rampaged. So now she fought him hoof against claw and horn against beak to end his fiery reign.

Pain arched between her limbs as the griffin's beak once again tore deep into her left flank and the unicorn stumbled. The griffin pounced onto her back and bit through her neck before she could recover. Her life flowed as a red river down the battlefield and into the thicket where her foal was hidden. The unicorn mare saw a twinkle of silvery white among the trees as her only offspring fled his dying mother.

***

The griffin dominated the Auleig forests and moors for many years while the unicorn mare watched from her spirit's place among the constellations. His harsh rule desolated the many populations living under his command. Many creatures rebelled against him, but all eventually joined the unicorn mare among the stars. Then, in the seventeenth year of the Sindon griffin's reign, a unicorn with silver hooves like his mother's came to challenge the mighty king. The unicorn's bold ambush caught his larger and stronger enemy by surprise. The griffin chased the impudent beast into the highest of the Auleig forests, seeking out his enemy among the red trunks of some rudha-an trees. As the old beast pushed his way further between their branches, his bulk became wedged between them. And as the brute tried to free himself, the unicorn stallion attacked.

"For my mother and my country!" the stallion cried as he trampled the griffin to death.

***

"Your Majesty? Your Majesty, please wake!"

Ina raised her head off the down pillow. The scents and sounds of the dream were still sharp in her mind as she looked past her maidservant to the narrow window of her bedchamber. By the wan light of dawn, she could see the tattered silver banner still flying high over the castle battlements—its white unicorn galloping fast upon the smoky morning breeze.

"We are still besieged, but not yet overrun?" she asked in a voice deep with weariness.

"Yes, Your Majesty," Rudha replied. "Auleig is safe for the moment, although the captain of the guard wishes me to inform you that the northern battlements are in a dismal state. The wall cannot hold much longer."

"The weakened left flank…" Ina whispered.

Rudha blinked in confusion.

"Where is my son?"

"The little dear is still happily asleep in his bed, My Queen. Even the battle has not roused him."

Slowly Ina sat upright and gazed at her maidservant. She noted the grim determination and courage in her fellow Auleigian's eyes as well as the weary lines etched along her face. "My dreams tonight were prophetic, Rudha. We will fall against the hordes of Sindon and I will not survive the battle."

"No, M'Lady, no!" Rudha gasped, her hand thrown over her quivering lips.

"We have little time. Rudha, listen to me." The Queen of Auleig stood and placed her pale hands on the other woman's shoulders. "I need you to take my son away from here. Keep him hidden and keep him safe until such time as he is ready to win back the kingdom. Teach him everything you know. Help him remember me."

"With all due respect, Your Majesty, you cannot be serious—"

"Among all my people, you alone are the most loyal and least self-seeking. You have served me vigilantly without complaint for nigh on twelve years and therefore it is you who is fated to carry out my last wishes and help my son destroy the Sindoni Empire. Raise Tristan in secret and teach him all the wisdom you know. Please, Rudha, will you do this for me?"

Rudha stared at her for a long moment and then finally bowed her consent. "Yes, Your Majesty, I will do my part."

Ina stepped back and curtsied to her own servant. She then turned, knelt, and tearfully kissed her sleeping son. "Goodbye, my beloved. Stay free."

The baby reached up to touch his mother's face before yawning and rolling over in his sleep. Ina moved the boy to a small basket and carefully tucked clothing and blankets around his tiny body to protect him from view. "Go then. Take Tristan and flee!"

As Rudha took her precious burden down the servants' stairs,

Ina walked to the narrow window. Fiery chaos reigned below her as the enemy's molten boulders pounded the walls.

With the help of two other servants she quickly redressed in her armor and left the safety of her chambers to seek out the captain of the guard. As she climbed the steps toward the battlements, however, a deafening explosion shook the wall and a horn bellowed the call of castle's breach. Ina staggered back to her feet and peered past the enemy's snapping griffin flag toward the distant forest. A lone horse and rider were climbing the hills beyond the bloody battlefield. As the rider and her precious basket finally slipped under the concealing shade of the pines, Ina smiled through her tears.

The Banner Prophesies:
A Parent's Ultimate Act of Love

I was sleeping in an Arizona hotel room when the first words of "Banner Prophesies" whispered through my mind. My husband had to stay in Nogales for six weeks on business and so I drove over 1,000 miles to keep him company one weekend.

I actually dreamt the scene between the unicorn and griffin late one morning. When I awoke, I had to scramble to my laptop before the dream dissipated back into my brain's groggy ether. Once the fight was written, I spent a couple of hours agonizing over where the story should go. My husband was at work at the time and all I could think about was the fact that I missed him. Somewhere in the middle of my frustration, I found myself wondering what it would be like to lose my husband permanently and the horror of that idea spurred me to write Ina's thoughts as she works to save her only son from their enemy.

I think Ina faces her own sacrifice of mortality with incredible courage. I can only hope that I would be willing and able to do the same if I had to make that horrific choice.

Winter Winds Blow

Why do cold winter winds blow
Over hills and dells of snow
And my faint fire flickers out
When my thoughts of you abound?

Melancholy are my dreams
As our lives split at the seams.
Words I scream to gray ceilings
Set my pain on angel wings.

Miss you now, I do the most—
Hearing each breath that you choke.
Silence greets me here most days.
Whispers gain my strongest praise.

Seeking meaning in your stare:
Are you still there enough to care?
I watch for a whiff of grin,
A lone tear, or snatch of hymn.

You squeeze my hand as I wait.
Was that intent or just strange fate?
I ask and you squeeze again.
Yes, you are still near, my friend.

A Song for Naia

We called the world's natives the Frozen since they were trapped in the secret places beyond our light. I know not how long they existed inside the glacier's cold shadow, but I do know that my people were the first to give them fire songs.

My first fire song after our landing lit the night sky with a vision of our ship's travel through the black void between our rotting world and this sea-blue jewel. The hardship of the journey was still evident in the char streaks along the ship's dented orange hull. The fire song was full of golden high notes symbolizing hope and I believe it was these notes in particular that woke Naia.

I heard her discordant plea inside my mind. "Come! Come! Recover me," it shrieked.

So I left the safety of our campfire with only my own kindled soul for warmth and sought the cold cave beyond our camp's radiant circles of light. It was there in the womb of the ice that I made my first memory of Naia's ethereal face.

She was the Frozen bound closest to the surface. Her blue-black countenance was caught in eternal terror, her six limbs were pushed up to protect her from the icy waves now solidly encasing her. She stared blankly until my fire-laced fingers touched the ice before her oval face. The heat of my song's passion melted the cold separating us and her green gaze met my glowing red eyes. Awareness awakened after many millennia and she seemed to recognize me.

"Oft have I craved the warmth of your touch, Ryad," her voice echoed in my mind while her look told me we would be lovers if I could free her.

Naia's and my combined songs sparked a kinship stronger than her bonds and her spirit's kindling soon awakened all of her people. The Frozens' spirit songs cast visions across the blue stars of my people's bright coming. In sleep they had waited for us, the Fire Singers, to leave our own scorched planet and melt theirs.

Now their spirits sing constantly in our minds. "Burn away our cold aloofness," they keen. "Your blazes, dear Embers, fuel our passion and thaw our icy abode."

"We two are equal parts, Ryad. Together we become balance," Naia's thoughts whisper inside me even as I continue to melt my way toward her freedom under the setting blue sun.

Each sundown renders our daily progress futile as the twilight temperatures refreeze our fire songs' work. Others of my people have given up and will not leave the radiant security of the campfires. They say there is no hope of ever freeing our destined lovers without ourselves being frozen to death in the process, but I say I must try even though I might die in the attempt. Many frostbitten Ember corpses have been consumed in our campfires as their Frozen partners' spirit songs die with them.

For Naia's sake I must succeed. As I was her hope in the beginning, now she is my hope to the end. Naia's love strengthens me and my fiery determination flares through the frost. Each cold dawn I give in to my passion and my flame melts more of Naia's icy prison. Yesterday I managed to free four of her limbs before my fire finally died. I know night's shadow will refreeze her inside the cliff, but the planet is warming and so is my strength. Unlike the others, I do not seek the refuge of the campfires at nightfall. Instead, I sleep in Naia's arms with a wall of ice at my back. This sacrifice of security is the only way I can sing through more ice each day. Though I risk death with each renewed night frost, Naia's calm song has kept me conscious and her body's peculiar process of convection has kept me from freezing. Forty days ago, I could barely free a hand. Yesterday, I liberated four beautiful limbs!

Maybe tomorrow I will free her, maybe then I will have my bride and she will have her groom. For now, I rest my spent form in her languid arms as night comes to freeze us in song's sleep once again.

"Soon will I free you, Beloved," I say and then we both sing for dawn once more.

A sharp crack suddenly reverberates around us and I feel myself falling even as I hold tightly to Naia's lithe body. In moments we are horizontal on the floor of the variegated blue cavern. The final burst of warmth leaves my body, melting the last icy shackles off her beautiful form.

"Freedom, precious freedom!" Her own song is pitched high in triumph even as mine fades to a bare hum. I feel faint, my mind grows…dim.

"Ryad?"

So beautiful my bride.

"Ryad!"

**

Warmth kindles my thoughts again and I stir against something soft and moist.

"I lost you, I almost lost you." Naia's thoughts sting with panic.

"I am here and I am well, beloved."

Naia's many limbs tightly embrace mine even as I burn away her tears with strength renewed from my people's campfire. My smile matches hers as I settle my head in her lap and hum to regain my strength. I hear murmurs from Rue, Condion, and other leaders of my people.

"Look here, Ryad and Naia are evidence of the planet's warming."

"Again we must endeavor to free the Frozen!"

"By all means, we must."

Naia looks around, her thoughts calmer and her lips parted in a wide smile. "Now, our hope guides others," she sings.

My smile matches hers. Maybe tomorrow I will have my bride and she will have her groom, but, for now, her spirit song paints a lullaby across the indigo sky as our peoples add their chorus of hope to her melody.

A Song for Naia:
A Trial of Frost and Fire

My favorite way to write is by typing at my computer with my feet propped up on top of the subwoofer under my desk. I can feel the gentle vibrations of soft soundtrack music through my bare feet as I contemplate each character and the subtle boom of the bass helps to set the mood for each scene.

"Song for Naia" is one of the few stories actually not written in this way. Instead, the story was handwritten on a yellow pad while I lay on our living room couch and watched a particular scene from a television series over and over again. The scene was little more than a shot of the hot sun rising over the earth's glistening edge as seen from space and yet there was something about that particular scene that compelled me to write a story about finding love and almost losing it.

I love the fact that the characters' love is symbolized by fire while the numbing ice separating them embodies their fear. The metaphor of fervent fire winning over debilitating ice is so powerful to me. Such a tale is always the type of story I love to read.

Incidentally, Naia's name comes from the word "naiad," a reference to the water spirits found in ancient Greek mythology. It's just something I thought readers might enjoy knowing.

Winter's Charge

If every story must have a beginning, then mine should start on the ice. I was born on the ice. I was raised on it. I learned to hunt while running over the crisp, clear crunch of it. I am constantly captivated by the purity of its whites and the bejeweled depth of its blue hues. As a boy, I once even lost myself on it.

Losing my way on the ice happened as one of my people might expect, in a blizzard. My clan had trekked west from our summer village nestled amid fields of the tundra's fading fire-weed toward the rocky hunting grounds on the coast. I was 12 years old, and this winter would be my first chance to hunt with the men of our village. I was so excited as I mushed my small dogsled alongside those of the adults. What kills would I make this year to help feed the Alawaeun Clan? Would I catch a seal or a beluga or maybe even a walrus? Surely I was brave enough and strong enough now to hunt all three.

Our hunting party left the wooden shelters of our winter village once the ice fields proved safe enough to sled across. We traveled along the snowy ground with the light of the midnight sun to guide our sleds and the waves of the Aurora to wash our dreams clean. I dreamt of many things during our journey, but the dream I remember most was the vision of Nanuq. I saw Nanuq robed in her magnificent white fur with four great stars of heaven encircling her brow like a crown. With one mighty paw, she held back the frothy waves of the green sea. The outstretched claws of her other paw kept the tremulous mountains from tumbling on top of her. And in Nanuq's lap an Alawaeun child slept the deep sleep of one at peace with the world.

I am not sure why I dreamed about the great white spirit bear.

Perhaps it was a type of premonition given to me by the Father Spirit. The clan elders all say that the dreams dreamt under the Aurora are some of the holiest and most important of our lives. I am not sure if I believe that to be true, but I do know that my dreams under the multihued waves of sky lights are always highly symbolic.

The blizzard that changed my life came soon after the third recurrence of my dream about Nanuq. Our hunting party had just entered the less-sheltered part of Mukluk Pass when the winter storm unleashed its full fury. A blur of white obscured the sun, and then darkness overtook the world. We fought against the swirling cold, our quivering lips as blue as the ice deep beneath our fur-lined boots. My father yelled for the rest of the party members to huddle ourselves and the dogs together, using the sleds as windbreaks.

As the storm worsened, my father and I dug trenches in the mounting snow to further protect ourselves from the biting wind. I heard nothing but the storm's fierce roar until a sound far louder and far worse shook the frozen ground around us.

"Avalanche!" my father yelled. I saw the word form in his mouth, but never heard it resonate from his lips over the awesome shake of the earth. Even so, he shoved me out of our crude igloo toward safety. Fear fueled my legs and I ran with abandon away from the colossal sound of shifting snow. I ran blind into the swirling darkness, using my ears to guide me away from the deadly waves of white. When a wall of rock appeared out of the blinding blizzard, I tightened the leather gloves around my fingers and began to climb. I scrambled up the craggy mountain while waves upon waves of snow crashed into the pass below me. The avalanche tumbled through the pass, burying anything in its way. I kept climbing, unsure of how high I should go to be safe. I climbed up and up and only stopped when my hands began to blister from the near-constant friction of gripping stone with leather-clad skin. I was high on the mountain now and, although I finally felt safe from the avalanche, the blizzard's bite was far worse since I was so exposed to the winds. Our clan elders speak of the wind as the touch of the ancestors' spirits. If that was true, then clearly these gusts were the slaps of ancestors from a rival clan who wished me dead! I had to find shelter soon or I would indeed meet death on this slope.

I found my temporary salvation in the form of a shallow cave on the leeward side of the mountain. It was little more than a hole in the rock. It was too small for a full-grown man to use, but just large enough for me. I shoved myself into the stony darkness and used the remnant twigs of an abandoned eagle's nest to keep the howling spirits at bay. The last of my strength ebbed and I curled up inside my fur parka to sleep a dreamless sleep.

I found not blizzard, but a sullen gray sky when I awoke the next morning. The world that I greeted looked so different from the world I had left. Parts of the pass had snow piled higher than the combined height of three grown men in several places. The snowpack's now lumpy surface was strewn with rocks and debris.

I found a much easier path down the mountain than my original way up had been. A good thing, since my hands were more sore than useful. I had checked my fingers for frostbite and gratefully found none, but it would take time bound in bandages before I could use them without pain. I searched and searched along the pass for our campsite and found only the splintered remains of a few dogsleds. I found four holes where three dogs and a man had managed to dig themselves out of the snowpack, but everywhere else I met the frozen dead chaotically buried in their new white tombs.

As I stared at the tips of one man's frozen fingers shoved above the blanketing white, I realized that I had fled in the opposite direction from the rest of our hunting party. That decision had saved my life yesterday, but now I faced the world without supplies, transportation, or the older men's protection. I doubted I would last the night.

I kicked snow away from a half-buried dogsled in the hope that I would find food for my stomach and medicine for my hands in the wreckage. I found a bit of dried salmon, but little else of use. I hunkered down amongst the shattered remains of my fellow hunters and slowly ate the smoky salmon spiced with the saltiness of my own quiet tears.

Darkness soon found me, but I no longer cared. I had tried to follow the surviving man's and dogs' tracks, but the night's winds had already erased them. Then I had decided to wait out the day to see if the surviving man and dogs would return. They did not. I tried to remember the way home, but could not. With no place to go, I huddled next to the strewn supplies of my wrecked dogsled and tried to build a fire from its splintered wood to help me keep warm.

I stayed next to the graves of my clan members long after the fire died, the temperature dropped, and the winds rose again. I was trembling so violently that I was sure I would break my chattering teeth before the end, but if I must die, then at least I would die alongside my kin.

A shuffling sound roused me from my fevered thoughts and I looked up to see a miracle materialize out of the starry darkness. The miracle came in the form of one of the most dangerous creatures an Alawaeun hunter can encounter: a polar bear.

I wish I could tell you that I behaved in a manner befitting my new status as an Alawaeun warrior, but I am ashamed to say that I did not. When I first saw the bear, I screamed like a woman. Meeting death was about to be far more painful for me than it had been even for my frozen clansmen.

As the bear moved closer, I shut my eyes and waited for the strong swipe of a paw to permanently tear my spirit free of my body. I waited and waited, but death did not come. Finally, I cautiously peeked with one eye at the world around me. My eyes widened when I found the bear simply sitting in the snow and watching me. Although I am no judge of emotions in animals, I remember thinking that she seemed quite sad.

"What are you doing here, young one?" the polar bear asked.

My mouth fell open in surprise. Surely I was dreaming. Surely the Aurora had given me some last wild vision of peace before death finally claimed me.

She repeated the question and I quickly sat up against the cold stone wall behind me. "How can you speak? What are you?"

The polar bear slowly shifted her head, studying me with an expression far different from any other predator's that I had ever seen. "I am your guardian…for now at least," she said.

"My father once told me the story of how the Father Spirit sent an orca guardian to save a warrior from drowning," I replied. "The orca used the warrior's fishing net to drag his leaking boat back to shore. I have heard the same sorts of stories about belugas and ravens, but never a polar bear."

"Never a polar bear…" The sadness seemed to deepen in her dark eyes. "It is true that my kind and yours are often enemies, but not even I will thwart the Father Spirit when he decides to favor one of man."

I said nothing.

"Come," she said as she rolled her massive body back onto her four large paws. "You need warmth and food and you will find neither here."

I crossed my arms in stubbornness and stayed firmly seated on the tumbled ice and snow. If it was even possible, she laughed when she saw my resoluteness. "Come, young one," she said to me. "Death has no purpose for you yet."

"What is your name?" I asked.

"Ukiuq," she said the Alawaeun name for winter. "You may call me Ukiuq."

I tapped my hand against my fur-clad chest in a traditional tribal salute. "I am honored to know your name," I said. "I am Ataniq, son of Tuvaurat who is chief of the Alawaeun Clan."

She bowed so deeply toward me that her black nose almost touched the snow beneath her white-furred paws. "I am honored as well. Ataniq...yours is a strong name. Now come before you further drain it of its power."

I took a step toward her and then stopped again in uncertainty. "Where are you taking me?"

"Home to your village, of course."

Reluctantly, I moved my shivering form to stand beside her. Ukiuq lowered her massive shoulders within my reach and I heaved my sore, hungry body into a riding position atop her back.

Together we trekked through the pass and out into the white ice fields toward the distant Aputyaq Mountains. We stopped once on our journey that day so that she could dive for food through a large seal's breathing hole. I ate the raw fish that she brought me before she caught and killed a young seal. We rested after her fishing expedition to let her pick the seal's fatty remnants from around her teeth and then wash the meal's gore from her fur. While we waited for her coat to dry, I used my small stone knife to salvage some seal fur for use as extra lining in my clothes. The result of my labor was hardly nice smelling since I had no time or tools to tan the skin, but the extra layering did help keep more of the winter chill at bay.

Ukiuq and I moved on with her walking and me riding astride

her shoulders most of the way. I was asleep during much of the journey, but I do recall being pleasantly surprised by the soft warmth of the polar bear's pale fur. I needed that source of comfort more than anything else at the time.

We must have walked for two or three days after the ice fishing event, but I cannot be certain. When I slept, I dreamed that the spirit bear Nanuq was herding my clan members together using me as her shepherd's staff. When I awoke, Ukiuq and I stopped again so that she could find me food. I ate leftover fish along the rest of our journey inland, while Ukiuq ate nothing. That worried me, but when I tried to share some of my fish with her, Ukiuq refused it and told me, "It is more important that you build and keep your strength than I, young one. I'll be well enough not to need food until the end of our journey together."

I shuddered when I considered the implications of that. Already I had become so accustomed to Ukiuq's presence that I could not imagine life without her. She was my guardian and I was her charge. She seemed a second mother to me and she talked to me like I was her cub. That thought sparked a question.

"Do you have cubs?" I asked, both excited and yet somehow afraid of her answer.

"Once," she whispered, her warm black eyes staring unseeing at the ice fields around us. "Once, a long time ago, I was just another bear...a mother with two cubs to care for. I cared nothing for the world of men until one of them killed my cubs, then I sought my revenge."

I stared at her old broken tooth and shivered. "What happened?"

Ukiuq closed her eyes and sighed. "I killed the man who had killed my young and then destroyed his father when he tried to avenge his son's death. I left an Alawaeun woman as a childless mother and widow that day, just as I had become." She shook her head. "My sorrow spawned hatred and my hatred only birthed more grief. My retribution against men displeased the Spirit Creator because, as much as He loves His animals, He loves His people more. He punished me. He gave me the gift of men's speech, prolonged my life, and then set me as guardian and guide to lost Alawaeun children until my time in this world is spent."

"So you came to save me?"

She bowed her head. "And so I came to save you."

We walked on in silence then while I considered what she had told me. We spoke little during the next few days, but when we rested I always found myself drawn to the soft fur of her side to huddle in sleep. Later I would often awake cuddled beneath her paws against the firmness of her stomach. The fierceness of her protection unnerved me a little, but it saved my life once the wolves came prowling.

The wolves appeared on the sixth day of our journey. We had crossed from the ice fields of the frozen sea and onto the shallow snow banks along the shore when the pack found us. We heard them before we saw them and the viciousness in their howls raised the hair on the back of my neck.

"We just passed into the pack's territory and they are not happy with our presence," Ukiuq said. She kept the tone of her voice calm, but I sensed her unease through the sudden tightness of her shoulder muscles.

I frowned. "Don't wolves usually leave white bears alone?" I asked.

She nodded. "I think there is more stirring here than what meets the eye. Whatever happens, promise me that you'll stay close to me and do just as I say, Ataniq."

"I will. I promise."

I slid down from her back as Ukiuq stood on her hind legs, sniffing the air and pawing at the whipping wind. The pack loped along the snowdrifts toward us. They ran spread apart with their heads down and their eyes narrowed. I frowned. Not one of them stopped to check the scents of the wind or even to mark their territory on a boulder. Instead, they encircled us and halted in unison well outside of Ukiuq's striking range.

The pack's leader stepped forward and growled. "What purpose brings you to our territory, Nanuq spawn?" the alpha male demanded.

If Ukiuq was surprised at the wolf's gift of speech, she did not show it. "The Spirit Creator commissioned me to deliver this one safely back to his village under the protection of the Alawaeun ancestors. I dare not thwart the Creator's will or ignore the ancestors' guidance and neither should you, pack leader."

The alpha growled. "We care not for your spirits, bear. We have our own to contend with."

"And it is they that sent you to block our path," Ukiuq surmised.

The big white wolf nodded. "Your presence here has angered the Juk Clan ancestors. We have come to ensure that you leave their sacred hunting grounds at once."

The polar bear's lips pulled back from her sharp teeth in a silent snarl. "The Juk Clan members have always followed their dark shamans, who are enslaved to the will of the Spirit Trickster. Surely you don't follow his leadership as well."

The alpha puffed out his chest to make himself seem bigger. "Take care what you say of the first and true Morning Star. It was he who gave us speech. It was he who gave us this territory. We are his allies even until death."

"Then we are at war, wolf." A long low roar issued from Ukiuq's throat.

The alpha's lips pulled back from his long fangs in a cold smile. "And so we are."

The attack came swiftly from all sides. The six howling wolves charged us at once. I had readied my small knife, but it never tasted wolf's blood. Instead, Ukiuq grabbed the back of my coat with her teeth and flung me into the air toward the nearest up-thrust of snow-covered rock. My sudden flight confused the wolves, some of whom broke off their attack of her to chase after me. I sailed between the stout snow piles flanking either side of the rock and jammed my knife into the packed ice clinging to the rock's peak. Using the knife's leverage, I hauled myself away from the three snapping, howling wolf jowls below me. My feet scrambled onto a narrow platform of stone. I could feel the rock tremble as the wolves jumped toward me. They were abysmal climbers though, so I knew I would be safe as long as I could keep my precarious balance atop the icy perch.

With me away from direct danger, Ukiuq turned her attention to her own fight on the ground. Her claws flashed and her jaws snapped as she bounded toward the alpha male, kicking snow into the eyes of his allies as she lunged for him. The alpha dodged the first swipe of her massive paw and circled low to avoid the second. Ukiuq growled. She viciously bit and then flung a wolf that had crept a little too close to her. The female wolf slammed into my boulder, causing tremors to run through the stone under my feet. I desperately held on to my perch as the snow suddenly shivered off the rock and onto the three wolves below me.

While the young female died and my attackers busily dug themselves out of the shallow snowdrift, a powerful swipe of Ukiuq's left paw made short work of a second wolf. When the three wolves guarding my rock finally joined the fray, Ukiuq bared her teeth at the snarling newcomers and then fended off another attack from the alpha male.

He jumped back as the other three rushed in to assault her simultaneously from the front and sides. She sprang forward and bit the head of one of her attackers—crushing his skull—before another managed to bite her left paw. She roared and batted the attacker away, but he had caused enough injury that she could not put weight on her mangled paw. Even with only three useful limbs, she kept fighting.

For a while the bear and the remaining wolves seemed at a deadlock. Then, as two wolves distracted her, the alpha male finally managed to circle behind her. He dashed forward as she fended off his allies and caught hold of her rump with his sharp teeth. She roared again and threw him off. The alpha male's mate circled close. She lunged for Ukiuq's shoulder just above the injured paw, but was not fast enough to avoid inadvertently colliding with the alpha male as the bear flung him off of her. Together the wolf pair tumbled across the hard-packed snow. With the two wolves momentarily stunned, Ukiuq closed in on the last. She cornered him as he stood snarling and trying to scramble up the base of my temporary refuge. I watched the two of them fight—circling, snapping, and lunging at each other—until I heard the sliding of small pebbles behind me. I turned to look behind me and screamed. The alpha male had climbed up the shallow backside of the boulder while Ukiuq was fighting the other remaining male.

"Ukiuq!" I yelled as I brandished my small knife. The alpha's bloody lips parted in a silent laugh as he saw the terror in my face. My guardian saw it, too.

"Jump, Ataniq," she roared. She turned, lunged, and finally caught her foe with a fatal bite to his neck. "Jump to me now!"

I did not jump so much as simply fall away from those wretched canine teeth. I summersaulted through the cold air and found myself suddenly sliding down the angle of Ukiuq's back to the ground.

"Are you all right?" Ukiuq asked me.

I nodded. The impact winded me, but I was otherwise un-hurt. Before I could get up, however, the alpha female was there. She charged us and Ukiuq shoved me behind her with her good paw before rearing and pouncing toward the attacker. The two met and their blood mingled as the wolf bit the bear's neck while the bear broke the wolf's forepaw. They separated and snarled at each other. Ukiuq charged her again and she backed off.

I leapt for cover as the alpha male sprang from the boulder onto Ukiuq's back. My scream matched her roar of agony as he bit down hard on the back of her neck. Ukiuq collapsed onto the bloody snow under the weight of the wolf, but regained her foot-ing.

The alpha howled his hard-fought triumph as he bounded from her back. Then I saw the polar bear raise her uninjured paw behind him. She brought it down across the middle of his back and his howl turned into a cry of pain. She dragged his strug-gling body toward her and bit down through his neck. The alpha convulsed a moment and then went limp as his blood mingled with that of his fellow wolves.

With her mate and the rest of her pack destroyed, the alpha fe-male retreated. She loped on three legs off into the snow beyond our sight, leaving Ukiuq and me alone among the dead members of her pack. While the last threat ran from us with her tail tucked between her legs, I began to clean my guardian's wounds with fresh snow. As I tried to bandage the polar bear's injuries; how-ever, she gently pushed me away. "No, Ataniq, you must seek refuge with your clan while the danger is less. Quickly go before darkness comes and the rest of the Spirit Trickster's allies find me. Go!"

"No, I won't leave you!" I cried. For the first time in my life I did not care when hot tears filled my dark eyes. I let my sorrow spill openly down my chapped cheeks. "I promised you!"

Ukiuq smiled wistfully then. "I was never meant to live by your side forever. But you...you must live long and well. You must live so that you may tell the story of the Father Spirit's favor shown toward you and your family through my rescue of you. Go. Go and do not forget how much you are loved, young one."

Tears were freezing against my exposed skin. "I won't forget you. I promise."

"I know. Be strong for me, Ataniq; show me the power of your name. Your clan's camp is just beyond that hill. Find your family and tell them all that has happened."

I gave her one last fierce hug and then I ran. I ran swiftly over the crunching ice and drifting snow until my feet were numb and my chilled breath burned in my throat. But, as I saw the flickering campfires of the village, I heard a single wolf's growl. I glanced behind me and my heart nearly froze with fear. The alpha female was loping on her three good legs, trying to catch up to me. I tried to push through my fear and fatigue to run even faster, but I knew there was little hope I could make it to the protection of my clan before the wolf caught me. Injured as she was, she was still much swifter than I.

I gazed at the village in regret and was startled by a strange sight. I saw my father standing beside our family tent talking to a clan elder. Father wore bandages on his head, but he seemed otherwise well. I blinked and looked again. Yes, he really was there! He must have been the other survivor of the avalanche!

"Father! Father!" I cried desperately.

He looked in the direction of my voice. "Ataniq?"

The wolf was snapping at my heels. "Father, help me!"

"Ataniq!"

My father grabbed his bow and arrows and then sprinted faster than I had ever seen him move. He bellowed orders as he ran toward me. Several men from our village yelled and readied arrows as the wolf and I drew closer to the first row of hide and wood homes. I saw the red-painted ptarmigan feather fletching of my father's arrow as it shot past my face and imbedded itself in the alpha female's shoulder. She yowled in pain, but kept moving. I pushed myself as fast as I could.

"Ataniq!"

I felt a sharp pain as the wolf's paw caught my ankle. I tumbled forward in the snow as two more arrows flew through the air above me. They struck the wolf and she fell over dead at my feet. Then my father was there. He pulled me out of the snow and threw his arms around my slender shoulders in a fierce embrace. "Are you hurt?"

I shook my head as we examined my leg. The wolf's claws had grazed the skin beneath my fur pants.

"Ataniq!" my mother called. She half-pulled me from my father's grasp to hug me. "How is this possible? How have you come back to us alive from the avalanche?" she gasped.

"A polar bear," I answered. "She brought me home to you." I then told them the story of my escape from the avalanche and of Ukiuq finding me in the freezing snow among the dead remains of our kin. I explained our journey across the ice together and the wolf pack's attack and finally my last run alone to our village.

My mother, who has a far more practical soul than my father, laughed heartily at my tale. "Oh, Ataniq, you make up such wonderful stories."

"It's true, Mother. The bear found me after the thundering snow killed all of those around me."

"We had given up all hope," said my mother. "However you came to us, I thank the Spirit Creator for this gift of second hope."

"You should, Mother, for he is the one who sent the polar bear as my guardian and guide."

My father just continued to stare at me. Finally he spoke, "What was the polar bear's name, Ataniq?"

"Tuvaurat, you can't seriously believe our son's story?"

He silenced her with a severe look and turned back to me.

"Ukiuq," I answered. "She called herself Ukiuq."

"The winter bear..." My father stared off into the swirling snow as tears crept into his usually stern eyes. "She saved you?"

I frowned at his sudden display of emotion. "Yes, Father. She battled wolves to protect me and killed all but the one chasing me."

My father was speechless.

"Tuvaurat, what is it?" my mother asked.

He frowned. "Ukiuq was the name of the white bear that killed my grandfather and his father, but then she rescued me from the sea when I was a youth. She was old when I knew her, so it could not be the same bear that rescued my son...it couldn't be."

Mother and I both frowned. "I thought it was an orca that saved you," she said.

"I lied," Father said quietly. "My father hated polar bears and forbade me from ever telling the truth." He shook his head. "Even after he died, I never wanted to. The memory of my rescue is...too painful."

I stared at my father in confusion during the awkward silence.

Could Ukiuq's story of revenge and recompense really deal with our family? If so, why was my father so unwilling to talk about it? I frowned at the bear-tooth talisman hanging from Father's neck and suddenly gasped in recognition.

"Father," I said as I held up his talisman. "Ukiuq has a tooth that is missing half of its tip. It's the same shape as this one you wear."

My father stared from me to the tooth and shook his head again. "Now she rescues my son from the snow and saves our family line once again. Ataniq, where is she?" his voice sounded somehow wistful and sad.

"She was too hurt by the wolves to come with me for the last of the journey here. She is dying, Father."

He stared silently at me a while, his face unreadable. "Come, Ataniq, show me where the bear has fallen," he said finally.

Father grabbed his bow and an extra quiver of arrows. Together we trekked out of the village with five other hunters on dog sleds to the place where the Juk Clan's wolf allies had done their worst. We found Ukiuq lying in a wheezing heap where I had left her.

My father motioned to the others to stay back while he approached the downed bear alone, an arrow nocked in his bow as he moved.

Ukiuq moved her head toward him when she heard him approach. "Tuvaurat, is that you? You have grown since I last saw you," she said between wheezing breaths.

Father's eyes narrowed as he drew the bowstring taught.

"Father! No!" I cried, not sure what was happening or why. I fought against the strength of the Alawaeun hunter holding me, but could not escape his grasp.

My father watched the bear a moment and then commanded, "Show me your teeth, Winter Bear."

Ukiuq pulled her bloody lips back in a snarl although there was no malice in her eyes. She only stared at my father sadly as he counted her teeth.

His fierce gaze stopped at her broken tooth. "It is you..."

She stared at him forlornly. "Did you really doubt it, young one?" she whispered.

"Why?" he shouted. "Why did you kill them, but save me? I broke that tooth and you wouldn't even fight back. You should have fought back! You knew that I got stranded while on the hunt to kill you. Why save me and then save my son? You should have killed us both!"

"My revenge for my murdered cubs cost your family much, Tuvaurat, but it took everything from me. I swore to the Spirit Creator that I would make right by your family even if you did not do the same for me. If you kill me now or even if you leave me to die on my own, my task is complete. In forgiving and protecting your family, I have rid myself of the hatred that entrapped me for so long. Either way you choose, Tuvaurat, I will die happy and free."

My father frowned at the polar bear over the tip of his drawn arrow as she closed her eyes in resignation and waited for death. After a long sigh, he finally let down the arrow and dropped his bow in the snow at his feet. Then my father did a truly strange thing. He actually sprinted to the bear's side and encircled her injured neck in his arms. Ukiuq gently returned his fierce embrace with her uninjured paw.

"I'm sorry," he said.

"I'm sorry, too," she replied.

On my father's orders, the men of our village lashed three sleds together and lay the massive white bear on top of them. The sleds creaked under her weight, but their framework held. We used all five teams of dogs to haul Ukiuq while the rest of the hunters jogged alongside their dogs or took turns driving the other two sleds.

Our eventual arrival back at the village caused quite an uproar. My mother was one of many who protested the bear being brought into the camp.

"If we treat her wounds, she'll eat the dogs and kill the lot of us once she's recovered!" Mother yelled, and many others shouted their agreement with her.

My father held up his hand for silence and the crowd immediately quieted. "I am chief of this clan," Father said. "If I decide that the snow guardian stays, then she stays and no one may dispute me. I will tell you all that twice my family line has come near to extinction and twice has this bear been our savior. First she saved me during the hunting accident of my youth when my boat overturned and now she has saved my son from avalanche and wolves. She has more than earned the right of protection and aid from this clan. Would you abandon her in her deepest need?"

Not one person spoke.

"Good, then treat her wounds and find her food. As for shelter, she shall share my family's home until she is fit to find her own den."

"As the chief commands," one of the hunters said. "Let us honor and care for this blessing of the Spirit Creator."

Together the hunters helped move Ukiuq into my family's own dwelling and there she stayed while the village's shaman oversaw her healing. It took many weeks, but the polar bear eventually found the strength to hunt once again. Once healed, she often accompanied the clansmen for their hunts across the crystalline ice.

As winter passed that year, I watched with a smile on my lips and a song in my soul as my clan members opened their lives to my family's bear guardian. Ukiuq became so beloved by our people that we renamed our clan Nanuqraqtaaq, which means "people of the white bear," in her honor. The miracle that had saved my father in the sea and had rescued me on the ice now became the proud protector of all of my people for all the remaining days of her long life.

Winter's Charge:
The Journey between Hatred and Peace

It was a warm, sunny, dusty day in October 2013 when the idea for "Winter's Charge" came to me. I was sorting through photos of glaciers from my husband's and my recent trip to Alaska when the simple concept of a polar bear rescuing a human boy from the arctic wilderness popped into my head. I could see the polar bear clearly as she stood strong in the swirling snow, looking every bit the powerful predator she was. The question of why such a dangerous creature would want to save rather than eat a human being so intrigued me that I felt compelled to write the story.

Two weeks of typing and I had the answer: a sick chain of grief and hatred would finally be broken by Ukiuq's sacrificial act. While the story is told by Ataniq, it really is the story of Ukiuq's and Tuvaurat's relationship as it is played out through their decisions concerning Ataniq.

Like Ataniq's trek through the snow and ice, this story was a treacherous yet beautiful journey for me as a writer. The tale came at a time when I was ready to explore the links between grief and hatred and to personally learn how forgiveness heals them both. At the end of my journey, I can feel forgiveness swirl around me as thick as the snowflakes in a blizzard. Who would have guessed that in the midst of the storms of life, I would find such peace?

You Are More

You are more than an addiction
You are better than a disease
How I long for you to see
The other side of free.

But in the darkness you must tarry.
In regret you need journey.
Only those in the deepest mire
Can truly taste hellfire.

Surely now your life's your own,
But it brings you little peace.
You were mother and daughter…
Sister, saint, and sinner.

Now your place is as beginner,
But if you, unruly weed,
Die to selfish desire each hour,
You'll bud anew, my flower.

Chosen Sacrifice

Dragons, lend me your speed," the emperor's winged herald whispered as she pumped her mechanical wings hard to avoid a craggy peak. The cold wind clawed at her simple brown robes, but Miya flew on heedless of the discomfort. She raced the waning daylight across the cloud-cloaked mountains and prayed that she would safely cross the Demon Realm's northern border long before Mother Earth consumed Father Sun.

Fear gripped her as she watched the fiery orb that was the dragons' home descend toward the horizon. How could she hope to survive if her enemies found her in the open without the aid of Father Sun's light? The human flapped her wings harder despite her increasing fatigue.

As she flew over a second outcropping, a sudden crimson flash illuminated the clouds around her and searing pain engulfed Miya's right shoulder. The winged human screamed and plummeted out of the gray sky as witch fire raced along her flesh and robes. High Priest Yoshiro's stern face flashed before her tear-soaked vision as she fell.

"Father!" the human screamed as moist billows gave way to unyielding stone.

As the mountain rushed toward her, Miya rolled her uninjured shoulder and flipped her wings open in time to avoid crashing headlong into its rocky precipice. Her efforts, however, could not save her from landing in the twisted little pine blocking an otherwise direct glide to the ground. The resulting snap of branches around her small body was sickening.

The dragons' chosen warrior dropped out of the small tree and groaned. She felt both grateful and furious toward the heavy cloud bank, which had extinguished the devouring flames and yet concealed the perilous mountains just beneath it.

"That was too close a dance with death," she panted as she sat up from the gray dirt. Her shaking hands rubbed her slightly swollen belly. "Far too close…"

The redheaded human gazed around the empty mountain-top, brushing strands of the scarlet symbol of the dragons' favor away from her face. She shifted uneasily, knowing that her sacred hair offered no protection here.

"The fiends must be camped on one of the neighboring summits," the imperial messenger murmured while pulling the medical supplies out of her pack.

A preliminary check of her limbs revealed many cuts and bruises yet no broken bones. Thanks in part to her nimble reactions, Miya's worst injury by far was the burn on her right shoulder and arm. Only the wailing wind greeted her gaze when she searched the narrow mountain rim again for assailants, so she set to work treating her scorched skin with an herb-soaked cloth.

She sneezed from the pungent mixture of frost powder, cape jasmine, and garlic, and then shifted her attention to some experimental wing stretches once the medicine had saturated her wounds. Her right arm and shoulder muscles burned with the slightest movement, but she still had flying capability. That was fortunate since she needed to finish binding her injuries and find a safer haven quickly or risk death by the claws of the emperor's enemies. After all, the now splintered evergreen could not shield her from the elements nor from unfriendly eyes.

Choking on the stench of her seared skin, Miya scrutinized the swirling waves of cloud broken by jutting peaks. Her slanted eyes searched wistfully toward the northwest for the comforting sight of Uki Mountain while her mind glimpsed the dragons' holy training temple perched atop the sheer cliff. It would likely take her another three days' flight through the heart of Oni's territory to reach the mountain monastery. Could she really avoid the demonic red ogre or his vile cronies that long?

A heavy thump disrupted her thoughts and she spun toward the noise already gripping her jo staff protectively. Another woman stood on the ridge. The dark-haired stranger was garbed in maroon and black robes that loosely mimicked a Miko's traditional red and white attire—grand garb compared to Miya's simple robes. The newcomer also held a staff similar to those used by the holy shrine maidens and carried a long katana sword at her waist. Despite the similarities, Miya knew this young woman was no Miko but a Kuro Miko—an evil shrine priestess who served the demons. Judging from the profane red tattoos glowing on her pale cheeks, this priestess held a high rank among her peers and was therefore extremely dangerous.

The stranger's staff suddenly erupted with witch fire, piercing the gathering gloom. Miya instinctively shrank away from the crimson blaze as the woman held the staff aloft.

"Who are you, Dragons' Chosen One? And why have you encroached upon these lands?" The woman's booming voice matched the power of her scowl.

Miya stood her ground, keeping her staff steady and her metallic wings half-open despite the discomfort both actions caused her. "I am Miya, a simple messenger of His Divine Majesty, Emperor Komei, and—"

"*Divine?* A tanuki raccoon-dog is far more heavenly and well-endowed than that impotent half-wit!" The priestess sneered and roared with laughter at her own quip. "But I should not be so uncivil. Do tell me what message the imperious fool sends to the demons?"

The priestess's mockery caused Miya's face to burn with a fury matching the staff's crimson flames. She glowered at her opponent, keeping her stance stable in the way Yoshiro had instructed her.

"My message is not meant for your masters, but for the emperor's servants in the town of Zhouling," she said, hoping that the half-truth would be believable enough to dissuade further inquiry. None but the emperor knew of Miya's true mission and she wished circumstances to remain such.

"You seem quite lost, little human; the line of flight between the cities of imperial Buhana and colorful Zhouling does not even graze our borders," the Kuro Miko snarled, her gaze darkening ominously.

"This I know," Miya answered bitterly. "I stand as a victim of foul weather and even fouler timing. Had I been able to avoid the storm over Dazuki Heights I would never have encroached upon the demons' domain. But, as it is, the winds have overruled my own desires."

The priestess frowned pensively, an act that revealed two tiny red horns poking through her hair just above her wide pale forehead. This woman was a hanyo half-demon!

"Your words ring true to my ears, but that alone does not grant you immunity against proper punishment," the demon half-breed growled. "As a fee for your impingement, I require a lock of scarlet hair plucked from your own head and presented to me within the gold box that you carry in your rucksack. In turn, I will grant you safe passage within the Demon Realms for three days so that you may complete your journey unchallenged. However, you must also promise never to return to these lands once you have passed beyond their borders."

The winged human stared at her aghast. The emperor's golden flute case was a treasured heirloom passed between emperors and their favored sons since the First Dynasty. To give it over to this pagan was unthinkable! Even worse, any powerful demon possessing even a single strand of scarlet hair from a Dragon Warrior's head could possibly taint the dragons' blessing imbued within it and thus curse the Dragon Warriors themselves. She could not betray the sole protectors of her people.

Emperor Komei's crinkled face swam into mental view and she remembered his last words. "You are our last hope...my last hope, Miya-sama. Go with the wind and may our dragon lords protect you and my greatest treasure from all evil."

If she bowed meekly to the hanyo's wishes, she and the emperor's seed might live to see the whole of her people perish. If she fought this evil, she and the child could both die and yet her people might still survive. Miya swallowed at her choices and studied the hanyo's signature black katana. She knew that sword. The emperor only gave such swords to truly powerful Dragon Warriors, so this monster had destroyed one of her predecessors to possess it. Miya's meager jo staff would be fighting that sword! She shuddered and then gathered a deep breath to calm herself.

"Would you accept the flute case alone as payment for my crossing?"

The hanyo growled, "I will not."

"If the flute case with my hair will grant me safe passage through this realm, then I will give it..." The gloating hanyo's pointed teeth gleamed in the dim light, hardening Miya's resolve. "However, such a gift will cost my people very dearly. I therefore offer this challenge to you. You may fight me with any one weapon of your choosing except the witch fire that could so easily singe off my precious hair. I will defend against you with any one weapon of my choosing.

"If you disarm me, I swear upon my sacred honor that you may take what you wish without fear of retribution from the dragons, their warriors, or the emperor. But if I disarm you, you will gain not a single strand from my head nor will you possess the flute box. I will keep what is mine and take your choice weapon as evidence of your defeat and your pledge of safe passage through the Demon Realms to my destination. Do you agree to this challenge and its rules on pain of dragons' blue fire and death?"

The demon half-breed stared speculatively at Miya, her yellowish eyes resting once more upon Miya's scarlet braid. Finally, greed seemed to subdue her caution. She propped her staff upright against a nearby ledge, its blazing fire giving light to the ridge even as the sun began to set.

"I accept your challenge and adhere to its rules on pain of dragons' fire. Firefang" —a wicked hiss filled the air as she drew the black-bladed katana out of its ornate scabbard— "is my weapon of choice."

Miya nodded grimly and tucked her metallic wings firmly against her back for added protection. "Very well…I choose my jo staff, Iresong, as my weapon. Any other weapon used during the duel will forfeit the win and the trickster's life."

"Agreed!" The hanyo smirked and launched herself forward with superhuman speed.

Miya's sturdy jo met and turned the katana's strong blow just in time. The uncanny sword's momentum carried it flat-bladed down the length of the staff, giving Miya freedom to immediately strike the priestess's face with the jo's blunt end. The half-demon dodged the strike and circled her blade low. Miya parried the attack, but felt the blade's tip slice her flesh nonetheless. The cut in her thigh was not deep, but its sting distracted her enough that her next movements were clumsy. The half-demon grew bolder at the sight of Miya's blood and easily blocked her attacks.

They fought until the sun's rim barely lit the mountains and witch fire began to gild the surrounding summits. Miya's shoulder ached and her left leg burned. She wanted this terrible trial to be over and yet her determination to protect herself and her child kept her moving.

"Remember your hips, Miya-sama." Yoshiro's patient voice spoke on the edge of her memory even as her foe landed a shallow slash across her ribs. "Your hips, not your shoulders, give you your power. Focus every move from the balanced foundation of the hips."

Miya nodded resolutely at the reminder and refocused her efforts in the face of the Kuro Miko's prodigious skill. In the end, the herald's endurance eventually proved superior. Miya feinted away from a hard blow and twisted the sword from the hanyo's hands. The fiend lunged after the sword as it clattered across the rocks, but was caught short by Miya's staff strike to her neck and left shoulder. The herald then retrieved the sword and pointed it and her own staff toward the coughing half-human.

"Do you yield?" the herald asked as she stepped between the hanyo and her fire staff to thwart any treacherous action.

"Yes." Miya's opponent panted and looked with sudden fear at her vanquisher.

The messenger simply nodded and pressed the point of the sword to the fiend's throat. "I have defeated you in combat, therefore your life belongs to me according to Heaven's laws. However, because you are an honored adversary I shall not kill you unless you wish not to bear in life the shame of defeat by my hand."

The priestess slowly shook her raven-haired head, her jade eyes locking on Miya's brown ones. "You are a great warrior and a Chosen One of the dragons; there is no disgrace in failing to overthrow you."

Miya smiled gently and allowed her opponent to rise. The hanyo bowed deeply and Miya returned the gesture, wincing as her ribs burned. "Well met, hanyo. Now, I must depart. I cannot be long delayed and Oni's crows will certainly see to it if they find me."

Miya's opponent stared hard at her a moment before speaking. "You need not concern yourself about the crows tonight, Miya. They are under my orders not to harm you."

"And how could you wield such sway over Oni's messengers? Are you one of his children?"

"Curses, no." The hanyo howled in laughter. "I am Oni!"

"You?" Miya nearly dropped the sword in her shocked disbelief. One of the realm's most vicious and powerful demons was actually a half-human woman?

"You choose your opponents well." The fiend grinned wickedly. "Or perhaps I should say foolishly."

Miya stared. "How is that possible? Do you change your appearance at will, then?"

The hanyo nodded, still smirking. Then her body seemed to flicker out of focus and a scaly red ogress taller than two human men suddenly stood in her place.

"Fortune smiles upon you this day, little messenger," the ogress boomed between long fangs. "You met me on my Turning Day, when my magic is limited by my human form. You defeated me before the complete setting of the sun. Now my powers are strong again and yet you still hold my life in your dainty hands. Were that not so, I would tear you apart and eat your limbs. But, because of the mercy you have shown me even in your victory, I shall keep my promise and allow you safe passage through my domain. A life for a life; my debt to you is thus repaid."

Miya bowed, suddenly aware of how close to death she had actually stumbled. "Thank you, Oni."

The ogress grunted and then watched as the messenger gathered her belongings. Miya felt the unpleasant sensation of Oni's eyes on her back as she wrapped her injured leg and torso and then hoisted her pack onto her bruised shoulders, shifting her wings to accommodate the load.

"Will you not stay, Chosen Warrior?" Oni asked and Miya swore she heard pity and regret fill the monster's voice. "You are the only woman ever to have the dragons' blessing and to train in their combat arts, yet you find no true acceptance among your own people because you are female. Your people's prejudices hinder you. Our beliefs are not so rigid here."

Miya turned to the demon on the mountain but saw instead the white sands of Uki Monastery's practice yard caked upon her adopted brothers' brown robes after their fights. Her robes were always the cleanest after each sparing session, not that the boys would ever admit it. Even now she could see the slight congratulatory smiles under their otherwise surly expressions. The vision faded to the imperial wing-granting ceremony and the emperor's slight bow as he awarded her a place among his most trusted winged messengers. "I would gladly sacrifice easy acceptance for hard-earned respect, Oni."

She smiled wistfully and then nodded farewell to the bewildered red ogress before leaping off the cliff. She soared high and, using the North Star as her guide, raced toward the silk-trading city of Zhouling. She would fly toward it until the last possible moment and then turn west. The journey would mean an additional half-day's delay, but she must accept this rather than risk raising the suspicions of Oni's spies by flying directly toward Uki Mountain.

The winged herald raced north relentlessly for two days and two nights with the half-ogress's vile flock as her constant companions. Only once did a bird try to peck her. She banked hard to avoid him and sliced her new katana straight through his body during his attack. The crow's comrades left substantial distance between their quarry and themselves after the incident. They departed only when she crossed the series of dagger-like peaks marking the boundary between demon and human civilization.

Finally relieved of enemy presence, Miya thought it safe to rest. She slept a full day in a sacred ugan grove south of Zhouling before she recovered enough strength to continue her perilous journey.

With Father Sun high in Heaven's courts, Miya once more vaulted onto the wind's back and soon she beheld the distinct blue tile roofs perched atop Uki Mountain's distinguishing fist-shaped outcropping. Miya felt hope and anxiety beat as one in her heart when she spied the grand temple she had once called home. She wondered if the emperor's instinct to send his pregnant messenger here was true wisdom.

"If Yoshiro turns me away as punishment for my unwed relations, we'll have no other place of protection left." She gulped down her fear and focused on each beat of her silvery wings as she neared the complex. When her sandaled feet finally touched upon the courtyard's sacred sands, shouting scarlet-haired monks raced to meet her from every corner of the complex.

"Where have you been?"

"You are overdue! We have looked for you for three days!"

"Are you well, honored Miya? You look so pale!"

"Enough! Enough!" she panted, almost ready to faint with exhaustion. "Take me to the temple high priest immediately."

"At once, Miya-sama," said one muscular man and quickly guided her to the old priest's quarters.

High Priest Yoshiro was a lean gray-haired man who was still fluid with both sword and jo staff despite his advanced years. Miya bowed low to her beloved teacher and adoptive father. He returned the gesture before ushering her inside and hugging her tightly. He guided her to a plush cushion before graciously pouring cups of aromatic tea and bidding her to relax.

"Shame, little Miya!" he said after she had finally quenched her thirst. "What delayed you?"

"My sincerest apologies for worrying you, Honored Father. A storm blew me off course and into the demons' lands. I had to battle Oni to regain my freedom."

The elderly priest began to laugh at his adopted daughter's joke, but his breath caught in his throat when she unstrapped the black katana from her pack and offered it humbly to him. "Your father's, I believe."

Yoshiro's wide eyes traced the familiar curves of the ancient weapon that had been stolen in his youth.

"How did you survive?" he asked breathlessly, holding the sword like a lost lover.

Miya smiled in triumph. "Oni is a hanyo! She was in her human form when I met her. I challenged her and was able to disarm her. Per our combat pact, I took her katana of authority as proof to her followers that I had defeated her. In exchange for my mercy in allowing her to live, Oni granted me safe passage through the Demon Realm."

"Fortune is indeed upon you!" Yoshiro reached across the low tea table to squeeze her hand. "The emperor will be greatly relieved to know you are now safe, as am I!"

"Indeed…indeed he will," she replied half-heartedly.

He gazed intently at her burned arm and then peered wildly at the torn rucksack behind her. "Daughter, what is the matter?" he asked, suddenly panicked.

"The flute box is gone, Father. I felt Oni steal it from the pack as I jumped off her cliff," Miya replied. "A true pity for that box was to be the emperor's son's first treasure upon his birth. I had not the strength to fight her again to recover it. I am sure she would have gladly killed me rather than keep our bargain and come away empty-handed. At least, she did not manage to gain a piece of my hair."

"Then your mission has failed," the priest said dejectedly.

"In-part, Teacher, in-part." Miya smiled sadly. "I lost the heir-loom, but succeeded in my true mission nonetheless."

Yoshiro frowned. "What do you mean your true mission?"

"My mission to come to this haven had little to do with de-livering the flute case. I am sorry for our subterfuge, but the em-peror swore me to secrecy about my true mission until I met with you in private. You see, the emperor's most beloved treasure lies not in gold or jewels…"

As she said this, Miya felt a sudden pain in her abdomen and gave a soft cry as her hand messaged her slightly swollen belly.

Priest Yoshiro looked sharply at her. "Little Miya, are you well?"

"Yes, Teacher, I am quite well now that we are finally safe."

He blinked in astonishment and then his face hardened. "You are with child! But…you are not married…"

She rubbed her belly again and nodded solemnly. "Honored Father, for the sake of our people, I gave myself to Komei. His seed and last hope of an heir flourishes in my womb. This is my reason for returning to you. The child and I need asylum from the emperor's enemies until he is old enough to succeed his father."

Yoshiro frowned. "My Empress?"

Miya sighed and shook her head. "No, Father, I am simply a concubine and when my time to nurture the child within these hallowed walls is finished, I will be no more important than any other imperial servant."

"Miya…" Yoshiro watched her in consternation.

Tears trickled down her scratched face. "With the birth of the emperor's heir, hope blooms once again for our people. That is what matters most, no matter my lot. May the dragons smile upon me for my diligence to our emperor. I know few others do." She lowered her gaze from his and watched her tears tap the bamboo floor. "I am so sorry. Please, please do not think less of me, Father."

She steeled herself for an elder's rebuke of an unwed mother as Yoshiro walked around the low table.

"No, honored Miya…" He smiled gently but sadly as he knelt, placed the katana on her lap, and drew her into a sheltering em-brace. "What matters most is that you are finally home with those who truly love and respect you. You may be the dragon's chosen vessel only in your youth, and the emperor's chosen blossom simply for a season, but you will remain my chosen daughter for eternity."

Chosen Sacrifice:
The Honor of Forgiveness

Chosen Sacrifice" was a difficult story to write. Essentially, it is my love letter to unwed mothers and their families. Over the course of my short life, I have known many women who have given their bodies over to passion instead of purity. Sometimes the result is simply a broken heart. Sometimes the result is the burden of an ill-timed baby. And very occasionally the result is a newlywed family. In all cases, my heart breaks for these women who must shoulder so much responsibility often at too young of an age. The simple strength and sacrifice of unwed mothers to become single working parents astounds me, but I also recognize that many of them could never do what they do so successfully without the love and support of their families. It is with these emotions in mind that I created the character of Miya.

In Miya, I wanted a character who prized honor above all else and yet had committed one of the ultimate dishonors within her society by volunteering herself as a concubine. While her motives for seeking the emperor's bed were pure, her actions themselves were anything but. As the emperor's pregnant mistress, Miya has been marked as forever off-limits to other men. And once his heir is born, the emperor will cast Miya aside as something no longer useful to him. Miya cannot marry and make a family of her own and so she follows the last option left to her: she runs back to the person she calls Father for help.

Even while holding the bargaining chip of Yoshiro's ancestral sword, Miya does not expect much. After all, who would love a whore? However, it is her father's forgiveness that rejuvenates her. It is his love that encourages her. It is his protection that sustains her. And it is his discipline that will continue to nurture her.

May we all be so blessed to have someone show such compassion to each of us.

Of Kelpie Lullabies

Blistering black winds whipped around Keiranna, clawing at her clasped cape as she crouched upon the Watcher's Rock. She slapped wild raven tresses away from her gaunt face and surveyed the scene below her again. Three times the sun had greeted her through the sooty clouds and still there was no sign of her quarry. She knew none but the bravest messengers would risk riding along the Split Spine Mountains and that meant a long time between decent horsemeat meals. She sighed and tried to ignore her surly stomach's complaints. Some days even starvation seemed a better choice than her usual fare of polecat.

"I wish my waking hours were as comforting as my unconscious ones," she grumbled to herself. She tried to sing the lullaby from the previous night's dream. "Boldly call upon the height, Battle cries throughout the night. Victory will come some way, If you can but hold 'til day…"

Her ears stung at the mockery her gruff voice made of the tune. Finally she gave up and glared at the Stone Spine's hot springs where the kelpies usually swam. Keiranna had mixed feelings about the horse-like creatures. They would joyfully kill her on sight and yet their nocturnal singing had been her only serenity in the years following her fae aunt's death. How many years had it been since the curse had made faes of all her family and enslaved them to this wretched land? Fifty years? Sixty? And how long since the last of her family had died in her arms and left her alone in the Split? At least fifteen years or was it twenty? Keiranna frowned at her lapse of memory. There had been a time long ago when she could recall everything and feel each remembrance acutely. Now she could recall faces but not names; the

148

warmth of her mother's embrace but not the love it signified. She supposed she had existed as a fae shadow of her former self too long to understand anything other than kill and eat when she was awake.

"Maybe I should try to sleep and never wake," she wondered aloud. "The kelpies' lullabies could sing me to my death then. That might be pleasant."

Distant dust churned up along the ribbon of road and Keiranna shifted slightly to retrieve an arrow from her quiver. She notched it and waited. As the rider and his galloping gray steed drew closer, she frowned. He had a second horse with him and it was not a pack animal. She pulled the bow tight and, after a moment's hesitation, let the bolt fly just off-center. The hissing arrow arced and found its mark in the extra mount's left flank, which caused the horse to buck with a frantic scream. The fae girl watched impassively as the rider fought the beast and then finally let go of the rein in favor of trying vainly to control his own finicky mount.

The wounded animal loped off in the direction of the tar pits as the rider went flying from his saddle. He awkwardly bounced on his rump across the ash-strewn canyon floor until he came to a spluttering stop next to a pile of bleached bones. Keiranna split the winds and glided smoothly down to the canyon floor some 50 meters below the Watcher's Rock. She stood with an arrow pointed at his back before the messenger could regain his feet.

"Do not ponder escape, messenger, for there will be none for you if you displease me."

The man spun around, gawking at her. "How did you…Who are you?"

"Keiranna of the Blacmann Clan of the Daoine Sídhe."

Surprisingly, he did not tremble at the sound of her name as all the others had. She could still smell his fear, but it was tempered by the stubborn resolve growing in his green eyes.

"I have come to parley with you and to offer the horse" —he motioned after the fleeing beast— "as a gift."

Her head rolled back as she cackled. "Who would be daft enough to send a valuable rider on such a foolhardy errand, stranger?"

"His Majesty, King Gayal of Aelmosé wishes that I negotiate with you, Keiranna," he said evenly.

Keiranna brushed her knotted hair back with her spidery fingers and studied the man a moment. The confident stance of his lean body matched the power in his melodic voice. He seemed somehow familiar to her, but his face prompted no memories. Should she kill him and be done with it? A man like this would make a fine meal and would be a nice change from the stringy carcasses she usually consumed. She kept her grim's-tooth-tipped arrow at the human's thudding heart, but relaxed the bowstring somewhat as her curiosity trampled her logic.

"What is your name, stranger?"

"Edwin of Hightown Parish."

She smirked coldly. "Very well, Edwin, what is it you wish?"

"I ask that you cease the hostilities upon Aelmosé riders and allow us peaceful passage through your clan's domain."

Keiranna's malevolent chuckle split the pebbles under their boots. "And why should I grant such a wish when your countrymen hunted the Sídhe and Fae clans to near extinction?"

"Because I can return to you that which was lost," Edwin said and carefully removed a leather pouch from his belt. He cautiously removed its magic seal with a word in Shee's Tongue and held the open bundle out for her inspection.

Keiranna drew a few steps closer with her bow still ready. She suspiciously peered inside the brown bag and gasped when she spied a smooth sapphire gleaming in the dim midday light. Even after three decades, she recognized it immediately by both sight and sound.

"The Stone of Creation!" she exclaimed over the gem's gentle hum.

She stared at it with longing. For years the sacred stone had been entrusted with her family until the vile sorcerer Ember stole it and used it to turn them from aes sídhe into sheerie traitors loathed by fae and sídhe fairies alike. The members of the Blacmann Clan were trapped by the sorcerer's wards and forced to live on whatever meat wandered willingly into the now volcanic Split Spine Mountains.

The sheerie looked at Edwin in awe. "How did you come by this?"

"If I tell you the story, you must promise not to harm me or my steed this day and allow us safe passage from this place once you and I conclude negotiations."

"None but a sorcerer can hold the bonds of that stone." Her eyes narrowed. "And I do not trust sorcerers."

He returned her stare. "You and I both know that a true sorcerer could wield this gem to rend you in two even if you are protected by grim's-tooth arrows and pooka cloaks. Yet here you stand uninjured. All I ask is that the same courtesy be extended to me."

She surveyed him and then his gray horse in speculation. Could he truly do as he said? He might have offered parley to her in case he believed others of her clan were alive and watching. If she revealed to him that she was alone, it would likely mean her destruction. But, then after all this time of numb existence, would death be so terrible?

"Do we have an accord?" Edwin asked. His mouth was set stubbornly, but she thought she saw a glimmer of gentleness flit across his gaze.

Keiranna looked at her would-be prey and again felt curiosity overrule her other sensibilities. Slowly she nodded her head. "Come with me out of this horrid heat and we will discuss your terms."

At her suggestion, Edwin hesitated.

She cocked her head to one side in bemusement and raised her arrow toward the center of his chest once more. "Do you truly believe you can choose to thwart my wishes and live? Even if you use the stone against me, other fae will come and surely destroy you."

Edwin frowned and swallowed slowly before shaking his head.

Keiranna chuckled then. "Come. There are worse things than me to contend with in this land. We must seek shelter before the other fae creatures hear the stone's song.

"Collect your horses quickly and do not worry. I would never allow harm to come to such a messenger of hope."

***

The trudge to Keiranna's cave hideaway was steep and treacherous to the inexperienced. While she had no difficulty making her way back toward her mountain home, Keiranna's captive and the two horses found steady footing sparse along the craggy landscape. Several times she reached out to steady Edwin as he grappled with the lame steed and each time he stiffened at her touch. Outwardly she appeared aloof to his reactions, but inwardly she began to wish he would not shy away from her so violently. The regret confused her. Was this what feeling was like? If so, she decided that perhaps it was better to be numb.

"How much farther?" Edwin asked.

The messenger's panted question turned her broods back to their environment.

"Just beyond that ridge up there," Keiranna replied before continuing her relentless reconnoiter of the area.

The sickeningly fresh-wind scent of a full banshee crossed her nose. Keiranna checked their flank again and signaled for Edwin to halt. Banshees flew along the upper reaches of these mountains and only descended when they needed to feed. They were of little threat unless one looked directly in the scavengers' eyes, but the fact that a banshee was so close meant that something else far worse was likely hunting them as well. Keiranna sniffed and waited.

As the banshee gave its first moaning wail, the sheerie's nose prickled with the new scent of dried blood on fur. The lame horse's blood smelled sweet compared to this rancid stench. Now that they had stopped, Keiranna could feel the steady rhythm of magic different from the sapphire's hum in the rock beneath her.

She drew her bow taught and whispered for her captive to draw a weapon of his own.

"What monster besides a banshee stalks us?"

She swallowed. "A Gwyllgi grim."

"Grim?" Edwin's eyes went wide and he drew a stiletto concealed in his riding boot.

"When the time comes, aim for its heart," she said.

"Before the fae hound finds mine, that is," he replied.

She nodded and motioned him forward. Together they scaled the steep precipice, ever mindful of their limited maneuvering space. Keiranna's nose caught occasional whiffs of the grim's stench—first behind them, then beside them—as it circled its prey. Her unease intensified as each new scent confirmed that the grim would outflank them and win the advantage of higher ground. She strained her ears to listen and heard nothing but the occasional wail of the banshee and the beat of her party-members' hearts. It was amazing and terrifying that a wolf-creature the size of a small pony could move so silently.

The fae beast's attack came moments after they crested the ridge. With a wrathful roar, the scarlet-eyed fiend descended upon them with fangs flashing. Edwin escaped the black brute's strike by the barest of margins and rolled to safety. The lame horse; however, was not so fortunate.

The grim's claws raked flesh from the screaming mare's spine before returning his attention to Edwin. Before either man or beast could move, however, Keiranna's bowstring sang with the liberation of an arrow aimed at the monster's broad black chest.

The enormous fae hound howled in agony and staggered toward Keiranna even as Edwin's slender knife pierced its left eye. A second scream from the grim was answered with distant howls of rage.

Keiranna cursed and loosed a second shot into the creature's chest. It crumpled just in front of her feet. She snarled at the beast and yanked her arrows from its now silent heart.

"Leave the horse and run!" she screeched. She grabbed Edwin by the sleeve of his chainmail shirt and sprinted toward the sanctuary of her den.

Another ghostly howl pierced the gloom and was answered by a chorus of seven or eight others. Keiranna hissed as she felt tingling vibrations of magic split the air. The hum of Edwin's magic gem had drawn the attention of the fallen grim's pack and now they were closing ranks around it. The first grim had been a mere scout. The pack's more dominant males would each likely be the size of a large horse and not so easy to kill.

"Edwin, if you have any ability to wield that stone, I suggest you work your sorcery now!"

"How many are coming?"

"I have heard the threat howls of eight, but there are likely more who run silently. We cannot hope to make it to shelter in time."

Edwin cursed. "So be it. I'll do what I must to protect us if you will do the same."

She snarled at him. "I may be a monster in the estimation of some, but I keep my promises."

He nodded. "Can you bear the sun's light?"

She hissed. "It is very painful for me to endure, but I can survive it."

"Good."

Edwin opened the sack carrying the Stone of Creation and pulled the humming gem into his right hand. The skin of a normal mortal would have scorched at first contact with the stone's power, but not Edwin's. The sorcerer held the stone aloft with calm purpose as Keiranna, his steed, and he charged around the last rocky ridge and out onto the flat ash plains just below Keiranna's clan's mountain hall.

The grim stopped howling abruptly as their quarry charged toward them. Even as the pack descended on the trio, Keiranna's bow sang with arrow after arrow unleashed toward the glowing red chests of her enemies. She had killed three and wounded a fourth by the time the pack members closed around them.

"Edwin!" she yelled as the nearest grim lunged toward her.

"Hold onto me!" he yelled.

She reached for his left hand and as she did so, she was swept away from the grim's jowls and swung onto the back of Edwin's steed. She clung to the sorcerer as his horse hurdled the line of enemies. A grim yelped as the steed's hooves met his spine and pushed off his back toward freedom. Keiranna stared behind her in disbelief as the horse galloped his way across the plains. They had jumped over a grim! No normal horse could leap like that, not with two people on its back!

For a moment, the pack members seemed just as surprised as she. Then they recovered and charged after their prey. The horse was incredibly fast, but the grim were faster. Four were dead, but nine still pursued them. From her position behind Edwin, Keiranna could not shoot her bow and so she watched with gathering horror as their hunters closed the distance between them.

"Edwin, they're almost on our heels!" she shouted.

"I can see the entrance, Keiranna. We're almost there! When I tell you, close your eyes!" he answered as they hurtled toward her late family's stone fortress. "Now!"

Keiranna shut her eyes as light flared through the gloom. Piteous shrieks and whimpers met her ears. The thud of magic ceased as the grim hearts nearest to her burst and then stilled. She heard the horse's hooves clip against hard stone and then echo inside a rock chamber.

"Keiranna! Help me move this!" Edwin screamed as he dismounted and pulled her from the steed.

She opened her eyes to see the inside of her family's meeting hall swim before her bleary vision. They had made it to safety.

"Keiranna!"

She stared in confusion at the man who was pushing against a boulder beside the cavern's entrance. The anger in a grim's roar snapped her to her senses and she helped Edwin roll the boulder along its track across the cave mouth just before the pack's last remnant reached them. Sounds of sinister snarls and scraping claws met their efforts, but none of the pack could get past the boulder.

Keiranna sank to the floor in relief and rested her head against the cool stone.

"Are you hurt?" Edwin asked her between heaving breaths.

She opened her stinging eyes and squinted at him as he knelt beside her. Like him, she was panting. She never panted. Keiranna frowned and stared down at her pale hands. They were less luminous now than they should be and they were trembling. Trembling? She felt fear coursing like glacier runoff through her throbbing heart.

"Keiranna?" Edwin reached to steady her shaking hands in his. His warm touch made her flinch. She felt heat flow through her fingers and a curious sensation flow through her mind. She pulled away and scrambled to her feet. Although her eyesight had finally cleared, it was now blurred with tears.

"Stay back!" she hissed at him in rising panic—panic that she was never supposed to feel. What had he done to her?

In the guttering light of the cave torches, Edwin's horse walked over to stand beside the sorcerer and nudged him with his nose. The man turned to rub the stallion's head and spoke softly to it. The poor mount now stood wet and quivering with cold. Edwin cursed and, as the sheerie watched, he walked the gray stallion over to the room's center fire pit and removed his bridle and saddle gear. The man searched the saddlebags until he found an earthen jar of blue ointment to rub on the beast's mouth and sores. As he did so, Edwin whispered again in the magical Shee Tongue.

The sorcerer's whisper grew to a murmur and then into a song. In spite of herself, Keiranna's eyes half-closed with relish at the peaceful tune. As he sang, he continued to dab and wipe ointment across the stallion's body. With each stroke, the horse's filthy gray coat became a spotless white. As Edwin's voice grew strong, it was joined by the horse's own voice. Together they sang a haunting melody that conjured memories of moonlit forests and still, clear waters.

Keiranna gasped and shrank closer to the wall. "A kelpie!"

Edwin nodded slowly—almost apologetically—and then patted the breathtaking beast affectionately. "This is Dewain and he has been my faithful steed for many years now."

She stared at the fae beast. If Kelpies were faithful in anything, it was betraying their riders to their deaths and yet this one had brought his two charges to safety. She had never known a kelpie to do anything other than entice their prey to ride them into the boiling waters of the Split Spine hot springs. The rider was cooked alive and the carnivorous kelpie then consumed the victim at its leisure.

No one could possibly ride one unless he had powerful magic of his own to help tame such a beast. She knew of only one sorcerer strong enough to ever have kelpies at his beck and call: Ember.

"Ember, you thief!" she snarled. She glared at the sorcerer who had taken the Stone of Creation from her clan and then used it to create the curse that had shaped the Split Spine Mountains and twisted her family into monsters. She recognized his face, but not his age. This man looked barely 30, far younger than the cretin she remembered in her nightmares. How had his body regained such youth?

"I am his son, Keiranna," Edwin said calmly as if reading her very thoughts.

"How could I be so foolish?" she screeched. Suddenly she longed to be on the other side of the stone with the grim pack. "The use of Shee Tongue to open the pouch...outside my own clan, only the one who cursed us would know that language."

"And his descendants. Very astute, Keiranna. For my sake though, I am quite thrilled that you did not make note of that earlier or I would probably have been fed to the grim." He chuckled.

"What do you want with me?" she growled, very aware of the solid stone at her back. There was no way that she could move it in time to avoid his attack.

Edwin took a cautious step forward. "You do not believe my intentions to be pure, biased as you are toward my family. I do not blame you for that, but please believe that I only want to free and restore you to your former purity. The sídhe-kin Clan of Blacmann has always been a proud race of warriors. Your ancestors became the guardians of the sorcerers' Stone of Creation because they were the kindest and most honorable of all the fairy clans—the only ones who could balance and check the mortal enchanters' power for the good of all..."

"Get to the point, Edwin—if that is indeed your real name."

The sorcerer looked honestly hurt by that.

"I have come to undo Ember's dark deeds, Keiranna. But I need the willing aid of a Blacmann member to accomplish such a task for the plague of his magic runs deep within this place. I know you are the last of your kin. I know your struggle to survive in this wasteland has been abjectly lonely. I have seen your tears many a time through my father's scrying glass—"

"Your father?"

The sorcerer sighed before speaking again. "As I said before, Keiranna, I am Ember's son. He raped my mother, hoping for a successor and instead..." Edwin's visage hardened. "Instead he sired his own executioner."

He walked purposely toward her now.

"Stay where you are!" she shrieked and readied her bow.

With an almost negligent wave of Edwin's hand, the bow splintered in two. "Do you truly believe that bolt would halt me, Keiranna, knowing now just who and what I am?"

She lowered her useless weapon helplessly, but continued to glare. "I am to trust a murderer?"

"With as many riders as you have left horseless in these badlands, are you really any better than me?"

She bowed her head slowly. "I did what I must to survive... to care for my family."

"You have no family left, Keiranna, nor do I. It is not right for either of us to live so alone."

She looked at him uncertainly and then at the kelpie, which had continued its haunting song throughout their confrontation. Her eyes widened as Edwin's strong tenor added words to the melody. "Boldly call upon the height, Battle cries throughout the night. Victory will come some way, If you can but hold 'til day..."

Edwin's warm hands cupped hers as he finished singing the song of hope from her dreams. A warmth spread through her body and tickled the edges of her memory. Her mind recalled the last hug that her father had given her before the curse descended. She remembered now, not just the warmth of his body and the scent of his clothes, but also the love in his embrace. It was the same love Edwin's simple touch now offered her. Inside her a dam of apathy finally broke and beautiful emotions chased through her soul in a confused and wonderful tumult.

"You had no reason to trust my father. This I know. But trust me as I trust you, Keiranna," Edwin said as he placed the Stone of Creation into Keiranna's hands. "And help me remake the world."

She gazed upon the blue stone and then back at the sorcerer. She believed every word he told her. The gem's pure light always revealed truth and so now it reminded her of dreams long forgotten. Keiranna recalled night after night of crying herself to sleep and yet always in her dreams she had heard someone whispering reassurance. The memories brought forth joyful tears.

"It wasn't just the kelpies' songs I heard. It was you," she whispered.

Edwin slowly nodded again but kept silent. She watched his features soften and then looked once more into the gem's depths, knowing that both honor and love had finally returned to her.

"To remake the world…" she said as she embraced him.

For the first time in years, Keiranna truly smiled.

Of Kelpie Lullabies:
The Choice of Redemption

I love working with mythical creatures because of the freedom they give me as an author. Using mythological creatures allows me the ability to explore different cultural archetypes and stereotypes without overtly offending anyone. Of the many stories I have written, "Of Kelpie Lullabies" is a perfect example of this technique. I created a deeply flawed heroine who longs for a normal life, but is cursed by corrupted magic to be a murdering monster. In the end it is Keiranna's choice to accept or reject love and forgiveness for her crimes that determines whether or not she can have the normal life that she so desperately craves.

The story itself may deal with sorcerers and magic, but I believe that most people can identify with its themes of grief, love, longing, despair, and forgiveness. For example, how many of you reading this are personally cursed with the mental slavery known as drug or alcohol addiction? How many of you have become so angry that you have harmed someone with words, actions, or even your own fists? Do you hate yourself for the wrongness of your choices or the weakness of your habits? Welcome to Keiranna's hellish life.

How many of you know an addict cursed with the need for a substance that controls her life? Do you weep for her or are you beyond caring? What about those who hurt you? Do you write them off as monsters too loathsome to love or do you cry for them all the harder? Welcome to Edwin's predicament.

Edwin could have turned his back on the monster he saw destroying others from a distance, but he did not. He saw her, all of her. He saw Keiranna's anger and her sadness. He saw her brutality and her fragility. In the end he reached out to her because he understood her pain and realized that it matched his own.

Keiranna does not rely on her own strength to save herself nor does Edwin. Instead they make the choice to help each other and seek aid from a power far stronger than both of them to accomplish that goal.

I ask you today, who is your Edwin and who is your Keiranna? What power do you rely on that is greater than yourself to remake your life and to remake the lives of others? I personally rely on Jesus Christ to help me love myself and love others, even those who the world deems monsters. It is Christ's love, his sacrifice, and his defeat of death that I cling to daily because I know that nothing besides his proven love is strong enough to dispel my darkness. The love of Jesus is my healing.

Acknowledgements

While writing in and of itself is a fairly solitary activity, this book was not a project created in seclusion. Lorelei Logsdon generously lent her expertise as the anthology's main editor while Eric T. Reynolds and Amanda Kimmerly were responsible for the edits of two of my previously-published short stories. Thank you for believing in me! I must thank all my beta readers for their help in making each story the best that it could be, but my special gratitude goes to Mary Garner, David Gray, Will Morton, L.W. Salinas, Matt Sears, Debby Zuehlke, and Dennis Zuehlke for their extra work to make sure my story plots made sense and my characters were interesting enough to keep later readers enthralled.

Thank you also to my incredible circle of family and friends who have taught me so much and cheered me through all. It was my husband, Matthew, who first encouraged me when I began pursuing this crazy writing career a few years ago. Through the many ups and downs of this complex process, he has supported me. My parents have also been a constant source of reassurance and wise counsel as have several members of my extended family and friends. Above all, I thank God for His overwhelming love and unfailing faithfulness, which have inspired and informed so much of my writing.

Finally, my readers deserve a huge round of applause for finding my work and telling others about it. Writing is a lonely journey when the fruits of an author's labor go unnoticed, so thank you all so much for joining in my adventures. May we have many more together!

Author Interview

What inspired you to write *Musings***?**

Early in 2013, I was organizing a few of my computer's short story files and I suddenly realized how many of them I had written, but not yet published. I began making lists of which stories I thought would work well together in a collection. After much trial and error, I had a good combination of stories and poetry ready to be professionally edited in early 2014. The project took longer than what I had anticipated, but it was worth the extra time to make sure that I had a solid anthology.

What influenced your initial decision to become an indie author rather than pursue the traditional publishing route?

I was in a unique position in 2014. I had received several rejection letters from publishers and agents over the full volume of *Skinshifter* as well as many of my individual short stories. However, I also had several beta readers absolutely loving my work and demanding more. I had experimented with independent publishing on an unrelated project, but saw little success with that book because I had no idea how to effectively market the material. I felt far more confident with *Musings* because I really know the work's intended audience: fantasy and science fiction lovers like me.

Rather than wait for some big publishing fish to catch interest in my writing bait, I decided to give my readers what they wanted: my work, now. I took the leap of faith to hire a professional editor and publish the book through my own company Purple Thorn Press. My goal in all of this is to give my readers as much quality reading as I can for the best price possible. How far will this experiment go? I have no idea. I only hope to entertain and inspire as many people as I can and financially support my family through my work.

How can readers tell you what they think of your stories?
I thrive on the communication from readers. I do happy-dances every single time I read a review. Please, please, please take the time to review not just my work, but every other author's story that you read at your favorite retailers' websites. Readers need each other's informed opinions to help all of us decide whether we want to explore certain works. Honest and fair reviews help keep the literary world spinning.

How can readers keep up with your writing?
Go to **AlyciaChristine.com** for all the latest updates as well as several awesome extras. I set the website up specifically for the enjoyment of my readers, so please visit! Read my blog, ask me questions, sign up for my newsletter (and its freebies), view my award-winning photography and art, and much more.

What is it about the speculative fiction genre that appeals to you?
I love fantasy and science fiction for their powerful ability to let me escape from the world around me. As wonderful as this world can be, I often just want to be able explore a completely different realm full of new cultures and unique creatures. Sometimes I really need the opportunity to spend a minute storming a castle wall or riding a dragon in between moving loads of laundry from the washer to the dryer. Reading and writing fantasy allows me to mix magic into the more mundane moments of my life, but it also leaves me grateful that I don't actually have to battle a harpy over the territory of my own bedroom.

How did you become a writer?
I was a terrible reader as a child. When I was in kindergarten, I came home from school every day and cried because I just couldn't make the teacher's patterns of letters make sense as words in my mind. To help alleviate my frustration, my parents enrolled me in special education classes to boost my reading skills and my confidence. During my homework hours, Dad

would read my textbooks aloud as I followed along while Mom corrected my English papers side by side with me. The combination of those three things vastly improved my reading and writing abilities. By the time I was 11, I could read college level material, but my speed was still three times slower than most of my peers. I hated reading because it was so difficult until my father stepped in once again.

During my summer vacations from school, Dad would read novels aloud to Mom and me as a fun way to pass the time. Every vacation or family holiday became a doubly-special event because each holiday meant a road trip during which Dad would crack open a new adventure. Soon I came to a point in which just reading along with Dad was not enough. In some cases I would actually steal the book and read ahead when Dad was tired.

Dad read books to me well into my college years and it was those stories that helped me realize a joy for reading that stretched beyond the tedious necessity of the classroom. My fondness for reading shifted into a passion for writing during my college career when I took my first creative writing and journalism courses as a sophomore at Texas A&M University. Suddenly I had the ability to actively participate in my own written adventures, not just read along while someone else's characters trekked around in their own world.

It wasn't until after college that I began to write in earnest. I wrote sporadically through the years occupied by my first three jobs—learning the fiction writing trade little by little.

Writing, like reading, is always an uphill struggle for me, but the reward of the adventure is always worth the effort of the journey.

Who are your literary influences?

Thanks to Dad, I grew up with Gordon R. Dickson's The Dragon and the George series, select books from Robert Heinlein, Robert Silverberg's Majipoor series, David and Leigh Eddings's Belgariad and Mallorian series. By way of more mainstream classics, Dad read James Herriot's *All Creatures Great and Small*, Baroness Emma Orczy's *The Scarlett Pimpernel*, and Mark Twain's *The Adventures of Tom Sawyer* and *The Adventures of Huckleberry Finn* to me.

In junior high (middle school), I discovered authors like Anne

McCaffrey, Michael Crichton, Frank E. Peretti, and Tamora Pierce on my own. In fact, Menolly, the main character from Anne McCaffrey's book *Dragonsong*, was the original inspiration for my *Skinshifter* character Lauraisha.

By scholastic necessity, high school saw me delve into more of the classics: Jane Austen, Charlotte Bronte, Emily Bronte, Lord Byron, E.M. Forster, Nathaniel Hawthorne, Ernest Hemingway, Rudyard Kipling, Edgar Allan Poe, William Shakespeare, and Edith Wharton. While I enjoyed some of Jane Austen's, Charlotte Bronte's, Nathaniel Hawthorne's, Rudyard Kipling's, and William Shakespeare's work, I detested the other authors. To this day, I will argue the validity of Ernest Hemingway's supreme writing skills with anyone in the room, but you won't ever catch me reading his work for enjoyment because I cannot stand being around his characters.

College found me happily adding J.K. Rowling and J.R.R. Tolkien to my personal library. I have read many other authors but Austen, Eddings, McCaffrey, Kipling, Peretti, and Rowling remain my go-to authors for excellent adventures.

Are there specific real life experiences that inspire your writing?

Absolutely. Part of the "Sumari's Solitude" plotline dealt with Sumari's relationship with her god Aa. I patterned much of that interaction after my own relationship with Jesus Christ. Likewise, the frost-bitten setting of "Winter's Charge" was directly inspired from seeing glaciers in Alaska. I actually wrote the story of "A Song for Naia" as I listened to a song from a TV show.

In my upcoming book *Skinshifter*, much of my writing deals with surviving and overcoming grief, which is something I think a person has to experience firsthand before she can try to explain it.

Just before I graduated college in 2005, my grandmother was diagnosed with cancer and died within a month of the initial discovery. Her sudden loss proved catastrophic for me and for my family because she had always been our strong center. I had written about two chapters of *Skinshifter* a year before her death, but I really wasn't sure what to do with the story. The calamity of Granny's passing changed that. It gave me new insight into grief and pushed me to better understand the nightmare that Katja endured when her own family and clan members were so violently taken from her.

My education in grief was expanded in late 2011 when my best friend of 20 years was struck with a massive brain aneurysm, leaving her with severe mental retardation and paralysis. She didn't die, but much of the woman I knew and loved is gone nonetheless. I was in the middle of writing *Dreamdrifter* (the sequel to *Skinshifter*) at the time, but I had to stop working for several months so that I had time to process all that had happened. When I began writing again, my typed thoughts had more focus and intensity than they had before Bekah's aneurysm. I was able to write scenes that I previously would have been too insecure to touch. The last half of *Dreamdrifter*, the story "Elza and Eliza," and the poem "Winter Winds Blow" came from that 2011 experience.

Rebekah was one of the first to read and encourage my written musings. It therefore seems fitting that I dedicate this book to her as a reminder of what a blessing she has been and continues to be to me.

Your older fiction is published under the name Alycia C. Cooke, but Musings is published under Alycia Christine. Why did your name change?

I published my first short stories under the pseudonym of Alycia C. Cooke for two main reasons. The first was the fact that I had published several journalism stories under my more complicated maiden name and I didn't want to confuse early fiction fans with a bunch of news articles. The second reason was that I wanted to write as Alycia C. Cooke to honor of my late Granny.

However, after many months of contemplation, I decided to publish *Musings* under Alycia Christine. After nine years, I think it is finally time let my grandmother go and completely be my own person just as she would want me to be. One way to do that is to publish all of my creative work under a name all my own. Since most people already know me from my Alycia Christine art photographs, it feels right to publish my fiction under Alycia Christine as well.

What is next for you in terms of writing?

There are so many stories I want to tell! Right now I'm putting the finishing touches on the novel *Skinshifter*. I can't wait for this novel to be published! I have wanted to share Katja's story with the world for almost a decade and I think it's finally time to unveil it. I have quite a few stories related to Katja's world of Sylvaeleth that have been bubbling to the surface of my mind in recent months. I also have a few unrelated tales brewing on my mind's back burner. In short, you should expect to see some more wonderful fiction soon.

Also by Alycia Christine

Skinshifter

Katja has a treacherous secret: she is the only werecat in her clan cursed with the ability to skinshift into a human during the full moon. If her deadwalker enemies ever discover her ability, it could mean not just death, but eternal slavery for her and her entire clan. At this time of war, a mage like Katja must choose to either try to hide her ability or seek sanctuary among more powerful mages. When the first option fails, Katja barely escapes the massacre of her clan. Now, with the help of some unlikely allies, Katja seeks sanctuary at the mages' Isle of Summons. But can she really trust her newfound companions or will their magic prove even more dangerous than her own?

Coming Soon! Find out more at **AlyciaChristine.com**.

Meet the Author

Alycia Christine grew up near the dusty cotton fields of Lubbock, Texas. She fell in love with fantasy and science fiction stories when her father first read Gordon R. Dickson's *The Dragon and The George* and Robert A. Heinlein's *Have Spacesuit—Will Travel* to her at age ten. Her love-affair with fiction deepened when Alycia took a creative writing course while attending Texas A&M University. After that class, she was hooked as a writer for life. Her subsequent B.S. degree in agricultural journalism not only helped to hone Alycia's skills with a pen, but also with a camera. Today she uses her skills as a photographer to capture the beauty of the world around her and add additional perspective to her fiction and nonfiction writing. Find her at AlyciaChristine.com.

www.ingramcontent.com/pod-product-compliance
Lightning Source LLC
Chambersburg PA
CBHW022122170626
46808CB00002B/814